# THE WORLD BENEATH

## JASON RUBIS

SEVERED PRESS
HOBART TASMANIA

# THE WORLD BENEATH

## ISBN: 978-1-922323-11-8

# PROLOGUE:
# MEXICO, 1930

Pedro would not have seen the man—or the thing chasing him—had he left his sister's home even an hour earlier. He had been helping his brother-in-law dig a new well that day, and once they struck water, there had been a celebratory meal to go with the loud cheers. Maria had never been the best cook, but the food was plentiful, as was the beer. It was good to sit and laugh with his nephews and nieces. One day, when he had saved enough money, Pedro hoped to have children of his own, and a home and a garden and a wife to cook him *tamales*.

Then it was back to his own village. His brother-in-law offered him a place to sleep, even if it was just a blanket on the floor. Pedro had been tempted, but he had work the next day. Better to get home. The desert was silent under the moonlight, the sand and rocks whitewashed—almost like the far regions of the earth where there was eternal snow and ice. Were there really such places? Pedro had his doubts, but the priest in the village—a learned man if there ever was one—had assured him it was true. Everyone knew priests did not lie.

As he walked, the ground grew rougher, slowly rising into foothills, and then mountains. The Cave was there, yawning like an open mouth, and Pedro gave it a wide berth, eyeing it distrustfully. There were strange stories about the Cave in his village—nothing so easily discounted as rumors of ghosts or monsters. Strange people were said to have been seen at night, milling about the cave's entrance. What it was exactly that was strange about them was something the stories didn't go into. A man in Pedro's village claimed to have walked a great distance back into the Cave's depths and seen strange, multicolored lights flickering far away in the darkness. He had insisted he had seen a city of some kind—but that was clearly nonsense. Who would build a city underground?

Still, when Pedro saw the thin figure shambling out of the Cave's mouth, it gave him a start. The figure was running unsteadily, weaving from side to side as a man would run when pushed past the limits of his endurance, yet still determined to keep running, as though his life depended on it.

Pedro was leery of getting too close to the man, but the fellow seemed to have no fear of him. Though he stumbled, he had seen Pedro and was making straight for him with alarming speed. Pedro stiffened, reaching down to grope in the dirt for a rock. He had no other weapons.

But nothing in the man's demeanor was threatening, only frightened. He pulled up short and lifted his hands, babbling in what Pedro only gradually realized was English. Pedro shook his head. The priest spoke some English, and had offered to teach him some, but he had refused, seeing no need for it.

The man was white, older than Pedro, and bony almost to the point of emaciation. He was half-naked, wearing only a sort of leather skirt around his bony thighs, and sandals whose straps reached to his knees.

"Please," the man said, now in Spanish. "Please, run. Go now! It…" He shook his head, searching for the right word. "It's behind me. It's coming!"

That was when Pedro became aware of the tremors. At first, he was more curious than frightened. He had never heard of an earthquake, so he had no idea why the ground might be shaking beneath him.

Then he heard the noises, and curiosity turned immediately to a fear that turned his bowels to water. It was a loud, animal sound, of a kind he'd never heard before. It thundered from the Cave's mouth, and it didn't need echoes to make it sound unnaturally loud. Whatever was making that noise was big—bigger than any animal should be.

"*Andale, andale*," the stranger muttered, pushing him back and casting fearful glances back at the Cave. "For God's sake, *run!*" The last words were delivered in English, but Pedro understood them perfectly well. He needed no further encouragement. He had no desire to see the thing in the Cave.

Then came a crashing sound, even louder than the roars, and despite his better judgment, Pedro cast a glance over his shoulder, even as he and the man sprinted together across the sand. Had the man not been pulling him along, he might have fallen to his knees, in sheer awe of the thing the earth had spat out.

It was *big*. Once, years before, an old man had come to his village with a ramshackle movie projector and a stack of films in dented canisters. Pedro had gathered with the others to see this curiosity. One of the films had been what the old man called a *newsreel*. It showed a number of different cities and people moving through them in vast numbers…and it showed something else that had struck Pedro as even more wonderful: a circus. The performers who swung through the air were amazing, but most incredible of all were the elephants. Pedro and his cronies had spent many an hour debating whether such bizarre creatures could be real.

The creature from the Cave was bigger than an elephant, and far more fearsome and strange. It ran like a gargantuan chicken on two vastly muscled hind legs, with two front limbs so tiny they were more like growths of some kind. A tail stretched out behind it like the rudder of a fantastic ship, and its head…

Its head was the worst thing about it—a gigantic wedge split by a mouth loaded with teeth, each as long as Pedro's arm. Tiny, evil eyes locked onto him and then the thing roared again, and with thundering steps came toward him.

This time, Pedro did fall, staring up at the thing with no will at all to run or save himself. He heard the stranger crying at him in both Spanish and English, urging him to run, but this thing was Satan himself, surely, or one of his attendant devils. How could such a thing be resisted by a man? It couldn't.

Suddenly, the stranger was in front of him, digging something out of his kilt. The monster was nearly upon them. All Pedro could do was stare up at the man's back.

Then things got even stranger.

The stranger lifted something in the air over his head, something that flashed in the darkness like a star. The monster stopped abruptly in its tracks, weaving a little and sniffing the air suspiciously. Whatever the thing the man had, the monster didn't like it.

Then the man was rising in the air, levitating like an Indian fakir Pedro had seen in one of the movie-man's other *newsreels*. His sandaled feet rose until they dangled just over Pedro's head, then he went even higher. The thing in his hands was flashing and the man was chanting something in a language unlike anything Pedro had ever heard. The monster roared at him, snapping its jaws—but more like a frightened, annoyed dog would snap, not a demon out of hell. Suddenly, it turned and, with unhurried but determined strides, made its way back to the Cave. It gave both men a parting glare, then disappeared.

But the man wasn't yet finished. He continued his chant and whatever he held flashed and glittered like a miniature sun. The tremors began again, but Pedro knew these weren't caused by the monster. Stones began falling from the Cave's roof, piling onto the ground at the entrance. Then, suddenly, the Cave's mouth collapsed in on itself, in a huge cloud of dust and falling stones. No one would be entering it, not ever again.

That, it seemed, marked the end of the stranger's strength. He fell—not gracefully this time. He dropped like a stone. Pedro scrambled to catch him—he was sure the weight would injure him—but he was ashamed of himself, now seeing his passivity as rank cowardice. The man's slight weight carried them both to the ground, but he proved to be surprisingly light. A moment later, Pedro stood with him in his arms, holding him like a child.

He now saw what weapon the man had used against the monster—it was a stone, slightly larger than a big man's fist. It wasn't gleaming or flashing now; whatever power was in it had died, leaving it as dull and black as a lump of coal. The man gave it a weary glance, then tossed it to the ground as though coal was all it was.

"Dead," he muttered. "*Muerte.*"

"I'll take you home," Pedro told him, thinking the man meant that he himself was not long for this world. "I have another brother in my village and my parents are there. We'll get you food, make you well again. You'll see."

"Food," the man said, sighing longingly and shutting his eyes as Pedro began the walk. It would take time, but he was determined to repay his savior. A moment later, the man opened one eye, his mouth bowed up in a somehow sly grin.

"This village of yours," he said. "Do they by any chance have any beer there?"

# ONE

*This manual labor stuff was a lot like going to a gym back home*, Dirk Bannerman thought. The first day wasn't so bad. In fact, you kind of got into it after a while—all the rhythmic up-and-down of the lifting and carrying, the half-assed camaraderie between yourself and the other peons, until you were close to actually enjoying it. You kept pushing yourself to go further, to ignore the sweat pouring down your face and the aching muscles, looking forward to the beers that would follow. It was sort of cool…in a way.

But the second day? That was a completely different animal.

Dirk's phone alarm woke him before the sun rose, and he immediately wanted to die. His body was revolting—in every sense of the word. When he tried to stand, he fell right back down again, flopping back onto his cheap cot with a banging shriek of springs. It was nearly five minutes before he could even think about making a second attempt. By then, his head wasn't spinning quite as badly, but his stomach still threatened to turn over every moment.

As he stumbled out of his room to the tiny bathroom he shared with the Grande's other tenants, his thoughts were grim. Most of the men who were working with him on Pezo's ranch were twice his age, or more. This gig wasn't a temporary stopgap for them to replenish funds, as it was for him. This was their whole life, a daily routine probably since they hit puberty, and most likely all they could look forward to until they finally dropped dead.

Thing was, if Dirk didn't manage to get his crap together, he might find himself in the same boat. End up a common laborer, just as his dad had always warned him he would. It hadn't started out this way. He had come down to South America with his inheritance and vague thoughts of starting a tourist guide business.

That had quickly dissolved into partying, until one morning he realized his money was all but gone.

He had pretty much burned all his bridges back home. Failure wasn't an option, but if there were any others, they didn't seem to be in evidence.

After hitting the bathroom and rinsing off in the grimy shower, Dirk changed and picked up the large plastic bottle of water he kept in the hotel's small communal refrigerator. Returning briefly to his room, he placed it in his battered cooler with the scanty remains of yesterday's lunch. Then, carefully locking his room's door, he went out into the dark streets. Luis and Juan Pablo and the others were waiting at the bus stop outside the hotel. They nodded wearily at Dirk; the other men ignored him. They looked even worse than he did, but he knew in his gut they were a lot stronger. They weren't going to fall over puking after a few hours of toil in the hot sun.

A few minutes later, the bus arrived and then chugged off, carrying them over the rocky dirt roads to Pezo's ranch. They rode in silence over the barren farmlands, but inevitably, Juan Pablo started getting chatty. As Dirk was seated beside him, the chatter was of course directed at him. Luis gave Dirk a quick glance of commiseration, then shut his eyes, intent on catching a last few moments of sleep before work started.

It was about the dogs, of course. With Juan Pablo, it was *always* about the dogs.

"They was *big*, man," Juan Pablo said, lifting his hands to show exactly how big he meant, which, granted, was pretty big. "Like *that*. And like, scary, man. Scary and *big*. Like pit bulls."

Dirk shrugged. "That's probably what they were." He had been through this conversation at least a dozen times now. The repetition had become almost comforting, like doing dialogue from *Holy Grail* with his buddies. Except this was in Spanish—he had gotten pretty fluent while he was down here, which was maybe the one good thing about his relocation.

Juan Pablo blew a derisive whistle between his fat, pursed lips. "Naw, dude, these weren't no pit bulls. They didn't have no *hair*, man. And their heads was shaped funny. Like...like..." His chubby hands flailed in the air before he gave up. "Like, just *weird*."

The encounter in question had apparently happened just before Dirk's arrival in Tacaraguita. Juan Pablo had been out walking somewhere outside the village and been set upon by the "dogs." The details of where he was and why he was there in the first place tended to change in the telling. Only the ending remained the same—the "dogs," whatever they actually were, had managed to chase Juan Pablo up one of the low, scrubby trees that dotted the area and had kept him there for some time. The farmer who owned the land had found him the next morning, snoring loudly, his bulk comfortably wedged between two stout branches. Dirk would have given money to see that.

"I'm telling you, they was just big dogs," Luis put in irritably. He was a lean, grey man with sharp, sour features. Pretty much the direct opposite of Juan Pablo, in other words. "They got all kinds of dogs now—don't even look like dogs some of them. I seen them on the TV. You were just drunk. Probably chasing the girls again," he added, giving Dirk a quick wink. Like most of the men, Luis was fond of Juan Pablo, as irritating as he claimed to find him.

"Naw, man, but listen...I ain't even told you the funny part." Juan Pablo's voice lowered. "You know what them dogs had on?"

"Jewels," Dirk and Luis—and at least three of the men in the seats around them—said.

"Jewels, man!" Juan Pablo cried. "*Big* jewels, like big as your fist, all around their necks."

"Like a collar?" Dirk asked.

Juan Pablo shook his head. "I don't know they were collars or what, man. But they were *big*. And shining. All different colors." This was the point where he invariably went silent, staring off through the bus's window. Luis grunted in satisfaction at the welcome quiet, wrapping his arms around his chest and shutting his eyes again.

Dirk settled his head on the back of the seat, unable, himself, to get to sleep. He tried to form in his mind a picture of Juan Pablo's "dogs," but as usual, he didn't get very far. He imagined a pair of unusually large pit bulls. He didn't have any idea why they would be hairless or—still more puzzlingly—wearing jeweled collars.

Outside the window, a pale sun was rising. Pretty soon he'd have to work. He shut his eyes.

*Joy, joy.*

\*\*\*

Work that day was not as horrible as it might have been. After some bad moments early on, he got into the swing of it, but his ability to adjust gave him little comfort. Marcus, Pezo's foreman, kept an eye on him as the work progressed. He had made it clear more than once the previous day that he didn't like having an American on the team. As it was, they needed as many strong backs as possible. Most of the younger men in town were already gainfully employed at the local silver mine. If not for that, it was doubtful Dirk would have been taken on at all.

Luis and Juan Pablo wordlessly offered to share their lunches with him, but Dirk refused, though by lunch time his hangover had worn off and he was ravenous, having eaten the little food he'd brought. He remembered his days as a barfly back in the states, how his friends had given him shit about constantly mooching drinks and cigarettes. He wasn't going to start that crap again with Luis and Juan Pablo, who had little enough food and money of their own.

By the time the bus dropped them off that evening, he felt ready to fall over again. He already knew the next day was going to be a bitch. He and Marcus had gotten into a glaring match late in the afternoon, and he was no longer sure how long he was going to be working at Pezo's, no matter how well he adapted.

After nodding goodbye to Luis and Juan Pablo, he headed into the hotel's bar. He knew he needed food more than beer, but he was dehydrated and, tired as he was, his nerves were jangled. He needed something to take the edge off.

It was a weeknight, so the place was quiet. Dirk slipped onto a stool and motioned at Gabriela for a beer. She took her time about it, shooting him glares with hard, coal-black eyes as she set up another order. She was a pretty enough girl, and fun to hang with when she was in a good mood; Dirk had instigated a little fling with her based on that, but she apparently had the idea he was in a position to immediately spirit her back to the States for a life of comparative luxury. When it became evident that wasn't happening, she hadn't taken it particularly well.

Before carrying a tray of drinks to the rear of the room, she slammed a cold bottle of the house's cheapest beer in front of him, along with a plate containing three *saltenas*.

"Left over from this morning," she said tersely. "You don't want them, I'll throw them out."

Dirk did, in fact, want them, and rather badly. *Saltenas* were Tacaraguita's breakfast (and lunch, and midnight snack) of choice—dense pastries stuffed with a thick filling of spiced meat, potatoes, and raisins. These were stale and cold, but they tasted just fine with the cold beer. By the time Gabriela sashayed back with her empty tray, Dirk had finished the beer and was licking crumbs off his fingers.

A moment later, the barmaid surprised him by slamming another beer down in front of him, this one of a much better quality.

"Thanks," he murmured, reaching for the bottle.

"Not from me," Gabriela snapped. She jerked her head at the rear of the room with a slightly unpleasant smile. "From *him*."

Dirk craned his neck, staring at the three occupied tables behind them. Trios of laborers sat at two of the tables, quietly drinking and seemingly lost in their own thoughts. A lone man was seated at the third table. It was hard to make out fine details, but he could see the man was not a laborer. The man lifted a bottle at Dirk in an unmistakable gesture of greeting and invitation.

Dirk groaned inside. *Great.* Part of the reason he'd failed as a businessman, he knew, was that much of the time he wasn't a big one for company. Not that he minded a companionable drink or three, but he liked to pick the time and place, especially when he was as tired and down in the mouth as he was now.

"Who is he?" he asked Gabriela.

"Don't know," she said, rinsing a glass. "He just came in this afternoon. American, like you. Maybe he just wants a younger man…for *company*." Gabriela gave him a malicious grin. There wasn't much doubt what she meant.

"Maybe he'll give you more than beer," she added under her breath. "A little money for your time, huh?"

That was enough for Dirk. Gabriela would keep on needling him as long as he let her. He knew she had reason to dislike him, and he wasn't proud of that, but he was starting to find this conversation distasteful. He picked up the beer and without a word walked back toward the man's table, feeling Gabriela's eyes bore into his back with every step.

Showing Gabriela up felt good, but as he walked, he started to doubt the wisdom of what he was doing. If that man's interest in him *was* more than just friendliness, going to him so readily could lead to further misunderstanding, or maybe other kinds of trouble.

*Well, it's too late now. Here we are. If we're lucky, we can just say hi and I can go back to my room and fall over, and that'll be that.*

"Just wanted to say thanks for the beer," he said, gesturing with the bottle.

The man smiled. Now that he was close enough to actually see him, Dirk found his appearance—more to the point, his outfit—startling. When he was a kid, he used to spend rainy Saturday afternoons watching old movies with his grandmother. This man reminded him irresistibly of some jungle explorer character from *Trader Horne* or one of the old *Tarzans*, what

Grandma sometimes called (for reasons completely lost on little Dirk) "Bwana Don" movies. Close-fitting khakis and high black boots. The only thing missing was a pith helmet and monocle.

He was tall and lean, with an unmistakably military bearing. His age was hard to fix, but his bushy mustache and carefully slicked back hair were snowy white. The eyes that regarded Dirk were blue and glittered with good humor and something like mischief.

"My pleasure," he said, gesturing at an empty seat before the table. "Please, join us."

Join *us*? There was a third seat as well, Dirk saw, and a third place set for dinner. The older man's plate was bare, but the third place was covered in crumbs and smears of red sauce. Whoever his dinner companion was had been eating, and apparently with some appetite.

"Don't want to intrude," Dirk mumbled, struggling to think of a suitable escape.

"Nonsense. They'll be back in a moment, and anxious to meet you." Before Dirk had time to process that remark, the man extended a hand. "Chalmers is my name, Theophilus Chalmers." His voice sounded like Old Money—but American rather than British, as Gabriela had said. Maybe Bostonian? Dirk had never paid much attention to accents before.

"I'm Dirk." Dirk shook the man's hand, impressed by the firmness of his grip. Then, not seeing any way out of it, settled himself onto the vacant chair.

"Will you join us for dinner?" Chalmers asked politely. "I eat little myself, but..."

"No, no, that's okay. I really should be getting back to my room...I have work tomorrow."

"Ah yes, Adam's curse," Chalmers said, picking up his own beer bottle and sipping from it. "May I ask what it is you do?"

"Just some farm work," Dirk said, coloring. As faintly comical as he found Chalmers, telling him about his circumstances was embarrassing, even humiliating. "Out on one of the local ranches. I'm kind of getting myself back together…"

"Of course, of course," Chalmers said, waving away his words as though the shame and worry behind them were of no matter at all. "One does what one can, of course. But what is it that brought you here? There are plenty of larger towns with rather more opportunities." There was none of the accusation in his voice that Dirk had long become used to in talking to older men. Chalmers talked to him like one guy chatting with another. It was kind of refreshing.

Dirk took a long swig of his beer to buy some time, a little surprised at the rich taste. It had been quite a while since he'd had anything so good. "Well, I had thought about being a guide for a while. I mean, that was big reason I came down here. There used to be a lot of tourists. You know, the dinosaur stuff."

Chalmers nodded, his eyes seeming to twinkle a little brighter. The barren countryside around Tacaraguita was known for fossilized dinosaur tracks. A few minor finds had been made in the local caverns as well. Several people Dirk had talked to back in the States had told him the area was a goldmine of rich American and European tourists, all begging to give their money to a knowledgeable guide who could show them fossils.

The reality had been quite a bit less impressive. The footprints were still there, but they were puny compared to what people imagined. The last archaeological digs had called it quits back in the '70s. The few tourists who came through town were less interested in dinosaurs than getting bargains on hand-made bags and rugs they could then sell in their expensive boutiques back home.

"A *guide*," Chalmers said, lifting his bottle and examining the amber liquid inside. He sounded almost rapturous, as though the idea were something so exotic as to be unheard of. "Yes, now *that* would be quite interesting, wouldn't it? Would you still be open to doing that kind of work?"

"What, a guide?" Dirk shrugged. He had a basic knowledge of the big "fossil" areas near town, having made a point of exploring them on his arrival. Apart from that, he knew he had little real experience to recommend him for the job. Then again, part of what had attracted him to the idea was the fact that, as he saw it, it didn't require much in the way of qualifications.

"I guess so."

"I may have a proposition for you, then," Chalmers said, leaning back in his chair.

Dirk looked carefully at the older man. This weird conversation had just gotten a lot more interesting. Chalmers didn't strike him as a skinflint and he seemed like he'd be agreeable enough to work for—more so than Marcus, certainly. A quick, well-paid jaunt around the local badlands might be just what he needed to get him closer to solvent.

Moving suddenly, Chalmers leaned forward across the table, eyes gleaming. "Tell me, Dirk," he said, his voice soft and somehow eager. "Have you ever heard of *Atlantis*?"

# TWO

*No. Oh, no. Oh*, hell *no*.

Dirk got up so quickly he had to grab the back of the chair to prevent it falling over. "Yeah, yeah, okay. That's…I gotta go, okay?"

He was awash in feelings of disappointment and irritation. *Atlantis*. Suddenly everything about Chalmers—the eccentric clothes and mannerisms—made sense. He was a crackpot. A loon, chasing fantasies out of old pulp novels. Whether or not he was a *rich* crackpot didn't make much difference to Dirk.

Cliff Murray, a guy he'd known back during his "I'm going to make a mint as a tourist guide" days, had warned him about rich crackpots. He had taken on a client convinced he was going to find Bigfoot in the wilds of Washington State…which was fine. Lots of people wanted to find Bigfoot. But this guy thought Bigfoot was a psychic forest guardian at constant war with a race of primordial tree demons. The further they got into the woods, the weirder the guy got, until Cliff was lucky to ditch him at a ranger station. He never did get paid. The story had made quite an impact on Dirk.

"Dirk, please," Chalmers said, extending a hand. He didn't seem overly agitated, which was good—the guys at the other tables were now staring openly at them, and Dirk had no doubt Gabriela was getting off on this scene in a major way. He looked, if anything, a little weary, as though this were a scene he'd seen played out again and again over the years. "You're misunderstanding me…I only meant…"

"Look, thanks for the beer, okay?" Dirk said, forcing himself to calm down. "You seem like a nice guy. But if you're looking for Atlantis out here in the badlands, I really can't help you. I'm sure if you ask around, you'll find someone who'll guide you. Probably somebody better than me, honestly."

He turned and headed for the door, head down to avoid the nasty chatter rising in the room and Gabriela's searching eyes. He was feeling sick about the whole thing. *Should've just gone back to bed. After this, I may never get up again.*

Before he could make his escape, Chalmers' voice rang out across the room, hard-edged and authoritative. "Please come back, Dirk. *Mr. Bannerman*. Please."

That stopped Dirk in his tracks, as Chalmers doubtless knew it would. He hadn't given the man his last name—he'd learned volunteering too much information was in general a bad idea. Maybe he was about to find out why.

He turned and stalked back to the table. This time, it was easier to ignore the voices and eyes. Bigger things were at stake.

"How'd you know my name?" he asked, keeping his voice even with an effort.

"Not through any sinister means, I assure you. Upon our arrival, I asked the natives for the names of a suitable guide. Yours came up over a couple of friendly beers. Another beer bought me your description and an idea of where I might find you."

Dirk felt himself calming down. The explanation made sense. "Sorry," he said. "It's just…" Just what? *Just that if you're interested enough in finding out my name, you could just as easily found out my parents' names and Googled up their address. Maybe sent a couple of goons to pay them a little visit late one night.*

At that moment, something like a small khaki hurricane came dervishing out into the room, moving with such force that Dirk felt himself pulling back in astonishment. For an instant, he wondered if a fight had started in the lady's room and spilled out into the dining area.

The hurricane stopped long enough to kiss Chalmers' cheek, then slip into the second vacant seat at the table and drink off half the water in its glass at a gulp.

"Oh my God! That bathroom is *unreal*! Oh my Lord, it was beyond *beyond*!"

The hurricane sat crunching ice cubes for a moment, regarding Dirk with huge green eyes, before saying, "Hello. Are you our guide?"

"Mr. Bannerman, allow me to present my granddaughter. She is accompanying me on this expedition as my assistant," Chalmers said. The old man was wearing a knowingly wry smile, as though Dirk's shocked reaction was something he'd seen many times over the years.

"Pliny Chalmers," the hurricane burbled, seizing Dirk's hand and pumping it energetically. "Charmed! What are you drinking? Grandpa doesn't like me to drink beer—he says it makes me giddy."

"Imagine that," Dirk breathed out. Pliny was about nineteen, he guessed—a petite girl, with brown braids that swung wildly with every new burst of nervous energy that overtook her. She was cute rather than beautiful, or even pretty, but Dirk found her impossible to ignore—if only because he was a little afraid of what she might do in retaliation. Her outfit was the same Great White Hunter type get-up as her grandfather's. Perhaps predictably, she actually *was* wearing a pith helmet.

"This is Mr. Bannerman, Pliny. Dirk Bannerman. He hasn't formally accepted the engagement as yet. I hope he will reconsider."

"No? But why not?" Pliny looked at Dirk as though his foot-dragging were a personal affront. "It's absolutely fabulous! We're making history! No, no we're *rewriting* history, isn't that right, Grandfather?"

"It is. Mr. Bannerman, I fear we've gotten off on the wrong foot. Please, allow me to start us off afresh. I'll just get us some refreshments. It's customary down here—as in many cultures—to begin a new venture with a full plate and glass. Very civilized, in my view." Chalmers lifted his head and signaled to someone at the bar. Dirk didn't have time to glance back and see if it was Gabriela who took the order. Chalmers was already off and running.

"When I'd mentioned Atlantis earlier, I apparently gave you the wrong impression. I only mentioned Mr. Plato's island by way of introduction to ideas much larger. The notion that a large prehistoric civilization, far more technologically advanced than we would believe possible today, influenced the development of other cultures, that influence spreading outward like ripples in a pond from a thrown stone." Chalmers waggled his fingers to illustrate. Dirk smiled woodenly.

"A very old idea, of course, well-explored in Scott-Elliott and a number of the Theosophists, not to mention dear old Colonel Churchward, of course. He called it Mu. Others insist on Atlantis, naturally, and yet others prattle on about Hyperborea and Xibalba. Most of them, of course, went in entirely the wrong direction. They insisted on digging through acres of splinters and potshards for signs of this primordial *ur*-civilization."

Chalmers leaned suddenly forward, eyes bright. "They all assumed it was wiped out virtually overnight. We can lay some of that at Plato's feet, naturally. But I put most of it down to their upbringing in a repressive religious environment that taught reaching for power was wicked, instead of man's natural state.

"My point—I'm sorry, I do a bit of prattling myself these days—my *point* is that it's highly unlikely such a civilization— with airships and lightning rifles and other marvels, would simply vanish in a puff of smoke. The Atlanteans—we have to call them *something*—may well have fallen on misfortunes, but they wouldn't have vanished. No one just vanishes. They would have gone somewhere. The question is, where?"

Dirk was beginning to regret not having run when he had the chance. Chalmers' tone was measured and eminently reasonable-sounding, but Dirk was growing more and more convinced the man really was a loon.

Perhaps fortunately, at that moment, Gabriela showed up with two fresh beers and a mug of *api* for Pliny, along with a plate of fried yucca chips and *saltenas* considerably fresher than the ones she'd offered Dirk earlier. She gave Pliny a sulky, contemptuous look as the younger girl dug happily into the chips, then shot Dirk a poisonous glare and padded back to the bar, swinging her hips all the way.

After the three had spent some time munching and sipping, Dirk sighed and said, "Okay, I'll bite. Where did the super-people go?"

Chalmers, beaming, opened his mouth. But it was Pliny who answered. "They went to an *underground* world! A cavern world, like Mr. Burroughs' Pellucidar! And you know what?" she asked, leaning forward as though her enthusiasm might prove infectious. "They're still down there!" She shot a worshipful smile at Chalmers. "And we're going to find them, aren't we, Grandfather?"

"I understand how this must sound to you, Mr. Bannerman," Chalmers said, helping himself to a single yucca chip. Apparently, he found the fact that Dirk had not run screaming this time encouraging. "A decrepit eccentric and his somewhat over-enthusiastic granddaughter, chasing ghosts in a poor, underdeveloped country. You may not be overly experienced as a guide, but I'm sure even you must see us as rather pathetic.

"But I assure you, this is no joke. Pliny, show Mr. Bannerman what I'm talking about, please."

Pliny, caught with her mouth full, was uncharacteristically silent as she reached into a leather satchel under the table, re-emerging with a battered-looking iPad. Moments later, Dirk was treated to a series of online news articles and blog postings about Chalmers and his ideas. Pliny swiped from article to article too quickly for them to be read in detail, but Dirk was able to get a quick look at most. Most had a definite "fringy" quality, but the writing and overall tone was altogether more sober than the ravings Dirk might have expected. The man in the photographs accompanying the articles was undoubtedly Chalmers, though dressed in a sharp business suit rather than his Bwana Don get-up.

"Here!" Pliny said triumphantly, pausing at one article. Her thumb hid the site's URL and most of the title and date. Dirk leaned forward and read a random paragraph:

*"Dr. Chalmers will be accompanied by his granddaughter Pliny, recently graduated from Harvard, in his search for an entrance to the underground world referenced in certain Vedic sources. A highly skilled team of scientists is beginning preliminary excavations in the fossil-rich regions near the town of Tacaraguita...."*

"Harvard, huh?" Dirk asked, looking at Pliny with newfound respect.

"Archaeology and anthropology." Pliny beamed, biting into a *saltena*. After some energetic munching, she said, "My doctoral advisor tells me I'm all but guaranteed a place on the faculty...once we finish this expedition, of course. But I'm not sure I'll be able to accept. There will be book deals, and I'm sure the movie people will be all over us...."

"Yeah, that can be a problem when you remake history."

She raised an eyebrow, but if she knew she was being teased, she didn't seem to mind overmuch. A moment later, her mouth was full again and Dirk took the opportunity to ask Chalmers, "So where's this team of yours now?"

"Presently, they're still on-site, beginning preliminary work," Chandler said. "They're in a cavern about a day from here, which I have reason to believe is the likeliest location for the entrance we seek." Dirk became aware that the man was watching him, carefully but unobtrusively. *He knows I'm thinking about it*, Dirk thought.

"And if you do find the entrance, what then?"

"Forgive me for appearing coy, Mr. Bannerman, but that is information I believe I should withhold for the moment. There is a certain sensitivity to this effort...."

"That's right," Pliny said, giving him a playful jab in the ribs. "You can read all about it later, while you count your fee."

"Alright, fair enough," Dirk said, not especially interested. After all, it wasn't as if they were really going to find anything, except maybe for some old bones and artifacts that would probably make them just as famous as a door to Pellucidar. "So let's make sure I understand: you just want me to take you guys to the site, is that it?"

"Not myself. Originally, my plan had been for Pliny and I to make the journey together, but certain business concerns of mine have made that impossible. It would be desirable to have someone knowledgeable about this area to see her safely to the site."

Dirk stole a sidelong glance at Pliny, who was obliviously slurping at her *api*. She caught his stare and grinned at him with a purple mustache.

"I know what you're thinking," Chalmers said quietly. "I'd be trusting you with a great deal. We are technically strangers to one another, after all, and Pliny is quite a young woman, besides being my only granddaughter. But you would not be alone. I have a younger colleague—you haven't yet made his acquaintance—who would, of course, accompany you to the site. And Pliny is not without resources of her own. She is, in her own way, quite a formidable young lady."

Pliny grinned enigmatically and mimed a small karate chop. "Hai-*ya*!" she said sweetly. "I believe you." Dirk smiled. "But you know—I'm just being honest here—I'm not exactly the most experienced guide in the world. I've never actually guided anyone anywhere."

"Yet I believe you to be both trustworthy and resourceful, like the far-traveled Ulysses. When engaging people, Mr. Bannerman, whether as a guide or a gardener, I look for a certain quality of spirit. You have that quality. I would, of course, provide all necessary gear. And I would pay you handsomely for what I believe would amount to little more than a day's work." He named a figure that made Dirk's eyes bulge. The temptation was now considerably stronger—very close to irresistible. The money would make his problems go away for a long time.

Chalmers must have seen the temptation in his eyes. "I can arrange to wire half of the money to whatever account you name, and the rest upon Pliny's safe arrival at the site."

Still, Dirk found himself balking. The thing seemed very close to too good to be true.

He shook his head. "I'd still have to think about it. I mean, this is sort of coming out of left field."

"Naturally," Chalmers said, leaning back with his hands flat on the tabletop. He was beaming as though Dirk had already said yes. "But I'm afraid time is a factor…you would need to leave tomorrow morning, and earlier rather than later. If you could sleep on it, and then inform me of your decision by, let us say, six AM tomorrow? You can find us here, preparing for the journey."

"Uh, but what are you guys going to do if I end up saying no?" Dirk asked. "I mean, that wouldn't leave you much time to find another guide."

"We'd just do without," Pliny said cheerfully. "Hari and I know the way—he's the fellow grandfather mentioned. We'd manage."

"Yes, I haven't seen many other men in town who would be suitable," Chalmers said. "It would be unfortunate, but with radios and cell phones, not impossible."

Dirk nodded, keeping his expression as blasé as possible. It wasn't exactly the answer he would have expected. The badlands were called "badlands" for a reason—they weren't likely to be gunned down by bandits, but it also wouldn't be like a quick jaunt through a shopping mall. Either these people were extremely naïve, or there really was more to Chalmers' proposal than met the eye.

Suddenly, Dirk found himself stifling a yawn. He had forgotten he had begun this evening in a state of near exhaustion. Any more thought on the old man's offer could wait 'til morning. He wished Chalmers and his granddaughter goodnight, shook hands with both, and headed for the door. As he passed the bar, Gabriela said, "Well? Did you and the old man have a nice talk?"

Her tone was light, but she was watching him with narrow, unfriendly eyes.

"Sure," Dirk said breezily. "He wants me to marry his granddaughter. Go up to Massachusetts and give him a whole flock of grandkids. Make me his heir. Can you blame him? I told him I'd have to think about it, though. Got a lot of other offers."

He made his escape before Gabriela could recover and throw a knife at him. He was probably mistaken, but he thought he saw her reaching for one out of the corner of his eye.

# THREE

Dirk woke in the middle of the night, his mouth so dry he had to spend some time working his tongue around before he could swallow. The snacks and beer—and the previous day's work—had left him dehydrated, as well as massively sore. He dug his water bottle out of his bag, only to remember he had neglected to refill it, as he usually did before bed. There was less than an inch of tepid water in the bottle. Groaning, Dirk got up and pulled on a pair of shorts, then went out for a refill.

The Grande wasn't much for amenities, but it did have a couple of ice machines. The nearest one, predictably, was out of order. That left the one on the second floor.

As he trudged up the stairs, he wondered what he was going to do about Chalmers' offer. On the face of it, he had little choice but to accept...unless he wanted to keep working on the ranch until either the work dried up or Marcus fired him. Still, the whole thing seemed weird. Beyond that, he wasn't sure he could spend a day without Pliny's chatter driving him barking mad. And the "man" Chalmers had mentioned accompanying them was another unknown factor. What if "Hari" were the anal-retentive type who had to feel like he was leading every enterprise he was involved with? That was exactly the type Dirk did not get along with. He knew he was unconsciously looking for reasons to refuse the old man's offer, but the late hour and his own exhaustion had made all the worst possibilities seem likely.

The ice machine was located just beside the stairs on the second floor. This was where the larger and nicer rooms were—typically, they went to tourists and people coming to see the dinosaur tracks, but they were largely empty at this time of the year.

*Then why*, Dirk asked himself as he pulled the lever that let ice cubes rattle into his bottle, *are there two guys trying to break into that room?*

They were several doors up from him, and there wasn't much doubt that the men in question were trying to break in. He couldn't tell much else about them. They were big guys, dressed in black, hunched over the doorknob, clearly trying to be as quiet as possible. *Maybe they were guests who'd lost their key*, Dirk thought, *or couldn't get the door to open for some mysterious but perfectly logical reason*. Not unthinkable. But the two didn't look like they would be roomies. For that matter, they didn't look anything like the hotel's usual clientele.

At the sound of the ice clattering, the pair started and turned toward him. Something about their faces struck him as strange, but at the moment, he couldn't put his finger on it.

*Leave it alone, Dirk. Not your business.*

"Just getting some ice," Dirk said, then added in Spanish, "No problem, okay?"

One of the men said something to the other—assuming he *had* actually said something; it sounded more like an angry hiss than actual words. A moment later, his friend was barreling down the hallway toward Dirk.

*Shit.* Dirk had two choices: either stay and fight or haul ass down the staircase. The results would probably be the same; he could only take the stairs so quickly and the guy was already on top of him. As a compromise, he made a quick feint toward the staircase, then whirled and flung himself onto the guy. There wasn't enough space between them to permit a solid punch, so Dirk grabbed his lapels and pulled, trying to throw him off balance.

What happened next made no sense. As Dirk tore at the guy's jacket, something seemed to flash under his shirt. In the sudden burst of illumination, he got his first good look at his assailant. His skin was beyond pale, more a greyish-white, like something you'd find growing under a rock. His head was bullet-shaped, with features so heavy he would have looked half-witted if it weren't for his tiny, startlingly sharp eyes. That wasn't the weird part, though.

It suddenly looked like he had a second, smaller head, equally sharp-eyed, but in no way human. The second head was pointed and reptilian with viciously sharp, forward-angled teeth. A long, stiff tail protruded from its hindquarters, tipped with a diamond-shaped blade of flesh. It hissed at Dirk, then seemed to separate itself from his host—not by tearing free but by unwrapping itself, then unfolding wide, bat-like wings that lifted it high above the grinning, pale-skinned man. It shrieked, then dove at him like a large, remarkably ugly falcon.

Dirk flung himself to one side, avoiding a direct hit from the winged thing by a scant inch. It came at him again and he snatched up his water bottle, throwing it. He got in a lucky hit, the sturdy plastic striking the creature's head with a loud smack and sending it tumbling to the floor with a scatter of ice cubes. It seemed considerably less at home on the ground, spreading its wings and jerking feebly as it tried to get itself aloft again. Dirk would have taken the opportunity to stomp the thing—if he weren't in his bare feet. Besides, its two friends were already on him, pulling him roughly upright. Dirk got in a good punch at the guy's ribs, but it was like slamming his fist into a side of beef.

*This isn't going to be fun*, he thought, gritting his teeth.

"Leave him alone!" a voice cried, high and somehow familiar-sounding.

At that moment, both of the men jerked back, crying out and groping at their chests as though both had been struck at once by twin heart attacks. The strange lights strobed off and on under their shirts, as though their torsos were bound with strings of blinking Christmas tree bulbs.

As they staggered backward, Dirk saw Pliny in the doorway of the room they had been trying to open. She was resplendent in a pair of pink pajamas, her scowling face smeared with some kind of makeup cream. She held in one outstretched hand what Dirk first took to be a fist-sized, irregularly shaped chunk of glass. It flashed with bright colors which grew steadily brighter in intensity, throwing the men's wildly struggling shadows on the wall. Whatever pain Pliny was causing them—by whatever means—it was clearly intense; Dirk's attacker broke down and screamed at one point. Their pet wasn't doing that well either; it lay squawking on the floor, its wings flapping miserably. Just before the screaming man snatched it up like a distressed pet poodle and tore off down the steps, Dirk caught a glimpse of small, multi-colored scales on its body, flashing colored lights in time with Pliny's stone. A moment later, it—and the two men— were gone. Dirk hurried over to the railing and watched the running shapes disappear out of the hotel and into the darkness.

"Did you *see* that?" Pliny squealed behind him. He could hear the regular thumping of her bare feet on the floor as she—was she actually *jumping up and down*?

"Was that a *rhamphorhyncus*? It had to be!"

*Rhamphorhyncus*. Dirk remembered sitting in a library, a picture-book on dinosaurs open before him. Eight years old, trying to spell out the long, strange-sounding names. He'd been crazy about dinosaurs back then.

"Wait a minute." He turned to Pliny—yes, she was in fact jumping up and down, still was. "You're saying that lizard-thing was a *dinosaur*?"

"Technically not a dinosaur." Chalmers' voice came out thin air behind him, making him start. The old man was still dressed as he had been at dinner. His mouth was bowed up in a grim smile. "A *pterosaur*, rather. A member of a very long-extinct family of flying reptilians. Still, *dinosaur* is a serviceable enough term. Not exactly in a classroom, are we?"

Dirk fought the urge to roll his eyes hard enough to make them bleed. "Fine. What's it doing here?"

"It's actually good news, though I doubt you'd think so if it had gotten those teeth into you. It's the first tangible proof that my theories are correct. If I'm correct, it's the first of many very unusual creatures we'll be encountering."

*That sounded good*, Dirk thought, *but so did pineapple on pizza*. He decided to switch tactics. "So who were those guys with it?"

"They are proof that our endeavors will probably be considerably more complicated than I at first thought." The old man turned to Pliny. "I'm afraid you'll need to leave earlier than expected, my dear. This place is apparently not the safe haven I thought."

"You mean we leave now?" Pliny asked, looking ready to start jumping again.

"Yes. Get your things together. I'll wake Hari." Turning back to Dirk, he said, "I'm sorry you were involved in that unpleasantness, Mr. Bannerman. I trust you took no significant damage?"

"I'm fine. Seems like your granddaughter had it pretty well under control," Dirk said wryly. "By the way, what's that rock she used to run 'em off?" Pliny, who had been examining the stone with great enthusiasm, abruptly slid it out of sight into her pajama sleeve.

"Naturally, I can no longer expect you to join us," Chalmers continued, blithely ignoring Dirk's question. "Of course I knew we might experience something like this, but I didn't anticipate it so soon. I could not ask you to put yourself in personal danger, which would be considerable. I will be happy to recompense you for the time you've already spent with us."

"Yeah, but wait…she's going to be okay, right?"

"Pliny?" Chalmers smiled. "As you yourself said, she has things well under control. And if she leaves right now, she'll be well ahead of any reprisals."

Dirk blinked. *Reprisals?* "You mean those guys will be *after* her?"

"Of course. If they are what I think they are—and they could hardly be anything else—they will indeed be in pursuit, probably with friends. But I'm afraid I'll need to cut this short, Mr. Bannerman. There's a great deal to do before Pliny leaves. I'll speak to the hotel's manager and see that you are recompensed for your time with us."

"I'm going with her."

The words were out before he knew what he was saying. To his surprise, he found he didn't regret them. In the years since he'd left home, he had seen some ugly things, most done by large, ugly men. Pliny might have some kind of magic rock on her side, but it was Dirk's experience magic didn't always come through when you needed it. The idea of Pliny facing the two men again made him a little sick to his stomach. More than a little, actually.

"I can't let her just go running off with those goons and their pet lizard after her," he said gruffly. "I couldn't sleep at night. I'll see her to your site, okay? Once she's there, your people can take care of her. Deal?"

He thrust his hand out and Chalmers stared down at it for a moment, a wondering expression on his face, as though Dirk had extended a tentacle instead of a hand. Finally, he took it, shaking it with the same enthusiasm Pliny had the night before.

"You live up to your surname, young man." Chalmers smiled. "And more than confirm my initial impression of you. Now go and get your things together. I can settle things for you with the hotel. You leave as soon as possible."

\*\*\*

"Hey, Hari!"

"Oi, Pliny."

"What's the best way to communicate with a *Spinosaurus*?"

"No idea."

"*Long distance*!" Pliny shrieked with delighted laughter.

"Ahhhh," Hari said, shaking his head ruefully. "You got me again! But here...Pliny?"

"Yes, Hari?"

"Why did the *Ankylosaurus* cross the road then, Pliny?"

"I don't know, Hari, why'd the *Ankylosaurus* cross the road then?"

"Because it was the chicken's day off, wasn't it?"

Dirk slogged along as far behind the two as he could manage, gritting his teeth at the resulting shrieks of laughter. Dirk would never have thought several hours of dinosaur riddles—most of which sounded like they'd been taken off bubble-gum wrappers—would be an effective means of torture. Now he would have happily confessed to the most heinous crimes imaginable, if it would have gotten his two companions to stop—or at least switch to knock-knock jokes. The heat and barren landscape they were walking through didn't help; neither did Hari and Pliny's constant laughter. Pliny's manic squeals were one thing. Hari's usual speaking voice was fairly deep, but when something really tickled him, he sounded like a damned hyena.

Chalmers had said very little about their companion, but something in his voice had led Dirk to imagine a tall, stony-faced giant in a turban, a keen-edged scimitar hanging at his belt. The reality was a little different. Dr. Hari Chandrasekaran had grown up in East London, and done most of his studies at Oxford, with some post-doc work in Texas. Apparently, his field was paleontology; he'd been a little cagey about details, but that hadn't worried Dirk too much—the man could have told him any imaginable lie about his work or background and Dirk wouldn't have known the difference. He was shorter than Dirk, but his bony build and quick, restless manner gave the impression of a much taller man. Dirk, to his relief, found the guy very likable; he seemed friendly and down to earth, with a ready sense of humor.

But those jokes…

"Hari…"

"Pliny?"

"What does a *Tyrannosaurus* eat?"

"Dunno, Pliny, what does a *Tyrannosaurus* eat?"

"Anything it wants!"

"Awwwww…!"

When Dirk saw the blasted-looking tree he had used as a marker on his last trip to the caves, it was all he could do to keep from whooping in joy. "Here," he said, possibly a little too eagerly. "We can stop here if everyone's ready for a break."

Pliny frowned. "Shouldn't we keep going? I'm not tired at all."

"But I am," Hari said, squirming out of his pack and giving Dirk a surreptitious wink. "Besides, the sun'll be at its highest point soon. Be hot as hell. We can lay up in the shade and hydrate a bit, then when it cools down, we'll take it easy the rest of the way. Hit camp in time to join our colleagues for a luxurious dinner of canned beans. That right, Dirk?"

"That's right," Dirk said. He was grateful for the support, though he was a bit irked at needing it. He didn't feel like much of a guide at the moment.

"But won't we be giving those men a chance to catch up with us?" Pliny asked. She had reluctantly taken off her pack, but it was clear she was playing her last card to keep them going.

"We'll be keeping an eye out. If they are coming, they can't really sneak up on us out here."

In fact, the possibility of pursuit had been weighing on Dirk's mind since they had left town. As they slogged along, he had constantly been glancing over his shoulder, half-expecting to see a truck or an ominous group of figures following them. But he'd seen nothing, and the land outside Tacaraguita was barren, with nothing much between them and the mountains in the distance; there would be nowhere for the pursuers to hide themselves.

The three settled themselves under the sparse shade of the tree, each taking a few swigs from their canteens. The heat, as Hari had predicted, was getting bad; still, it beat the hell out of moving boulders for Marcus. At the moment, Dirk almost felt sorry for Luis and Juan Pablo.

All well and good, but he still didn't intend to really relax until Pliny was safely in the hands of her grandfather's team. The cavern where they were holed up was a spot of only minor interest in the local dinosaur-hunters' guidebook. Not enough fossils had been found there, and its comparatively smaller size made it more interesting to spelunkers than tourists. So far as he was concerned, that would make it as good a spot as any to hold off an attack. Which might never come…

"So," he said finally. "Are you going to tell me who those guys were?" He was speaking to Pliny, but keeping an eye on Hari. He had a feeling the thin scientist might have more information than Pliny, but he had buried his nose in a tattered paperback and didn't seem to be listening.

"The truth is, we're not exactly sure," Pliny said, pulling a bag of trail mix from her pack and munching away. "Grandpa was getting strange phone calls since he announced the expedition."

"Calls? You mean like threats?"

"Yes. Very vague, but unmistakably threats nonetheless. But he had expected that, more or less. There are all sorts of odd people out there, you know. Religious fanatics who think we're engaged in some kind of blasphemy that contradicts their belief systems, or just mad-bad-sad types who watch the news looking for people to harass."

Her voice trailed away. Dirk said, a little irritably, "Right, but flat-earthers and young earth creationists don't carry pet mini-*pterodactyls* around. And you didn't hesitate when you pulled out that magic crystal of yours."

"Better tell him what we know, Pliny," Hari said, not looking up from his book. "He's got a right to know, if he's come with us this far. Keeping him in the dark isn't fair, and it could be dangerous if things get heated, yeah? Besides, what we do know is little enough."

Pliny gave him a sour look before filling her mouth with a fresh handful of nuts and raisins. "So we don't actually know…but we *think* they're from the inner world," she said, a little indistinctly.

"What, the place where the Atlanteans went?"

Pliny tried to reply, but a larger-than-expected cashew sent her into a fit of coughing. Hari offered her his canteen while he pounded her back.

"That's right, more or less," he confirmed. "Sounds daft, doesn't it? I thought so, when Theo—Dr. Chalmers—told me about it. But it makes a bit of sense when you think of it. If I were living in a highly advanced subterranean civilization, I'd want to keep an eye on the mad bastards living and loving and setting off nukes on my roof. You've probably heard stories about Lemurians living on Mount Shasta, coming into the local towns in their nightgowns to barter for supplies. Or men in black suits showing up when someone sees a UFO or the odd Sasquatch. That's a bit more like. If *I* were a Lemurian, I'd wear something a bit sharper than my nightgown. A nice well-cut suit, say, like the Kray Brothers. Nothing too flash, mind."

"And the inner world has living rhampho…rham…."

Pliny sniffed. "*Rhamphorhyncus*. Apparently so, because we saw one. Maybe more interesting things as well. That's what we're trying to find out."

"Okay. And that magic crystal of yours? What's the story there?"

He had just gotten to "magic crystal" when the shadow swept over them. It was startlingly wide, blotting out the little pools of sunlight filtering through the tree's dead branches, as well as the hot bleaching expanse on all sides for a good minute or more. For that minute, it was as though they had jumped ahead a good five hours to early evening, even though the air hadn't grown appreciably cooler. The blistering sun returned only to be blotted out again seconds later. Whatever had cast the shadow was circling them.

Pliny and Hari's response was considerably stronger than Dirk's. Dirk, taken by surprise, was just confused, but Pliny was already digging in her bag, presumably for the "magic crystal," and Hari had scrambled to his feet and was staring into the sky. He was crouched slightly, something in the way he held himself suggesting he was fighting an instinct to run.

"Oh, Christ," the scientist muttered. "I don't believe it. Fucking *Garuda*."

# FOUR

Whatever a *Garuda* was, it was big. When Dirk joined Hari in looking upward, his first impression was of a dragon with vast, outsized wings, at least thirty feet wide. But none of the dragons in the fantasy novels he'd read as a kid was as ugly as this thing— it more than outdid the little *Rhamphorhyncus* in that department. It had a long, toothy beak, balanced in back with a bony crest that nearly matched it in length. It was white and hairless, its belly covered with clusters of flashing lights that gave it an oddly mechanical appearance, as though it were some kind of robot rather than a living thing.

"Don't run," Hari breathed, grabbing Dirk's hand. "That's what it wants. If we leave the shelter of the tree, it'll be on us like a hawk on a mouse."

The thing circled overhead, letting rip with a deafening call that was half honk, half a strangely inorganic shriek, like a huge sheet of metal being torn in two. Dirk had the idea the thing was frustrated at their refusal to come out and be eaten. Each new pass brought it slightly lower.

By now, Pliny had managed to unearth the stone from her bag. She struck the same pose she had at the hotel, holding the crystal to the sky, her face contorted in a frown of concentration. *Anime chick rampant*, Dirk thought, fighting back a burst of slightly hysterical laughter. In response, the *Garuda* circled back and made another, lower pass over them. The resulting blast of displaced wind wasn't quite enough to knock them over, but it made it necessary to hold onto one another.

The three of them coughed, Dirk fighting back a wave of nausea. The wind from the thing smelled rancid, like something from a shallow grave.

Pliny cried out and clapped a hand to her head, as though in pain. "It's blocking me!" she said. "Nothing's ever done that before!"

"Don't use it again," Hari said. "They knew we'd try the *mani* again. They're prepared this time. They won't just block you, they'll throw back anything you send with triple intensity. It could destroy the stone…" His voice trailed off, but Dirk could imagine what he left unsaid easily enough—*or it might kill you.*

"So what do we do?" Pliny demanded. "Just wait for it to go away?"

"Sounds good to me," Dirk muttered. He didn't like saying it; it felt too much like rank cowardice. But there were worse things than being a coward. Being torn to shreds by a giant mutant possibly zombie *Pteranodon* ranked pretty high on his personal list.

"Let's just wait a minute," Hari said. A moment later, he cried out and yelled, "Get down!" The three of them flung themselves full-length on the stony ground as the *Garuda* made another, even lower, pass. This time, its crystal-encrusted abdomen scraped the uppermost branches of the tree, and its foul smell took a while to fade. *I wonder if it's too late to go back to Marcus*, Dirk thought. *I could write him a letter of apology, maybe bake him a cake…*

"Okay, we can't stay here," Hari said breathlessly. "I don't think it'll land; it'd be too difficult for it to maneuver on the ground…"

"But pterosaurs *can* get around on land," Pliny said. "They fold up their wings and sort of creep around on them…"

"As I was *saying*," Hari continued, with a patience Dirk could only admire, "if it does land, I wouldn't give us a very high chance of getting away."

"Call your grandfather," Dirk urged Pliny. Why hadn't they thought of that before? She had her phone…surely she did? *If not, I'll lend her mine.*

"And tell him what, exactly?" Pliny asked blithely.

"I don't know! Tell him we're being attacked by something out of *The Lost World*. Tell him to send in the freaking cavalry!"

Pliny managed to get her phone out but a moment later, she shoved it back into her pocket. "Dead. It's always hard to get bars out here anyway, and I'm sure those guys aren't helping. The *mani* stones are probably messing up the signals too."

"Dirk, you see those trees over there?" Hari asked suddenly.

"Yeah," Dirk said. He could see them—though they looked more like shrubs from here. "But they're too far away, Hari. We won't…"

"Take Pliny. Just get her there. *Just run.*" A moment later, he snatched the stone from Pliny and scrambled out from under the tree. A second moment later, he was standing upright on open ground, waving the stone and whooping.

"Oi! Big boy! Fancy some Indian takeaway? Little curry for ya? Come and get me while I'm hot, love! I don't reheat well!"

"What the hell?" Dirk whispered. He had never witnessed a suicide being committed before his eyes before. The *Garuda* swooped over Hari, and the paleontologist barely missed being snatched up in its claws. The thing came back, but even though, as Pliny said, the stone's power was now blocked, it still seemed wary of it. Hari ran as fast as he could back the way they'd come, laughing and waving the stone around over his head.

"Come on!" Pliny screamed, grabbing Dirk's hand and pulling him out from under the tree. They left their packs behind but that didn't seem to bother Pliny, so Dirk didn't give it a second thought. He kept snatching glances over his shoulder as he ran. He hadn't really, sincerely prayed since third grade Bible Study, but now he was praying Hari would make it to shelter before the *Garuda* got him. But by the third glance, he was an agnostic again. The creature squatted before Hari, its huge, ungainly wings folded up with tips well over its head, just as Pliny had predicted. It raised its head, tilting it back like a hammer about to drive in a stubborn nail. Dirk turned away before that final blow was struck, grateful that Pliny hadn't looked. She was concentrating on running and he did as well.

The distance between them and the stand of trees seemed immense, impassable. Dirk was sure that at any moment the flapping of the *Garuda*'s wings would sound overhead. Then would come a foul wind, a shriek, and sudden darkness. But he kept running until his sides ached, and by the time he and Pliny reached the trees, the looked-for attack had not come.

They crouched together, both streaming with sweat, looking at the *Garuda*. Even in the distance, it still looked enormous. It was prodding at something on the ground with its immense beak.

Pliny made a gasping, wordless noise, and Dirk saw she was sobbing. He couldn't blame her. He himself felt sick to his stomach, on the verge every minute of losing his breakfast.

"We'd better get going," he said finally, touching her arm. "We can make it to the mountains if we hurry. There'll be places there to hide. From there, we can get to the cavern and…"

"We could kill it," Pliny said, her voice fierce.

"Excuse me, *what*?"

"Look at it. It's vulnerable now. I told you, the big pterosaurs could walk on land, but not easily. And it'll have trouble getting airborne again." She picked up a fallen branch, one end a nasty, jagged edge. "We'll have the advantage."

"You're crazy," Dirk told her flatly. "I don't care if that thing is a quadriplegic or if it's doing the goddamned Watusi. It'll kill us."

"Hari died for us," Pliny said. "We owe him that much."

"But it's a *dinosaur*," Dirk said, mentally calculating his chances of overpowering her and simply carrying her off over his shoulder like a latter-day Alley Oop. So far as he could see, the odds of carrying this off were decidedly not in his favor. "Don't you want to *study* the damned thing, or something?"

"Wait," Pliny said. Her body had tensed and she stood leaning forward a little. At that moment, she looked oddly feral. Suddenly, she pointed. "What's that?" she cried.

At first, Dirk didn't realize what she was pointing at. Then he saw them: a couple of small pale figures milling around the *Garuda* and the still shape of Hari's body.

"What the hell?"

"Riders," Pliny said. "Don't you see? It makes sense. I thought they were controlling the *Pteranodon* from somewhere else, using the *mani* stones. But they were riding it, steering it. Making sure it didn't slip their control long enough to eat poor Hari." She shuddered.

"Yeah, but why would *they* want his body?" Dirk asked. Pliny only shook her head, and Dirk didn't push her. He was just glad she had dropped the idea of a full-on attack on the monster.

"Come on," she said finally, turning and starting to walk. "We have to make it to camp and let Grandfather know what happened. He's going to be *furious*," she added, scowling.

Dirk stared at the pale figures working away at Hari's body. It was impossible to see exactly what they were doing, but they didn't seem to be in any hurry. Recovering their packs would be impossible right now—and unnecessary if they could make it to the camp, where there would be food and supplies.

But if they couldn't, it wasn't going to be pretty.

Sighing, he started after Pliny.

\*\*\*

"Oh my God," Pliny moaned.

Dirk had nothing to add. They had made it to the cavern just as the sky was beginning to redden. Without their packs weighing them down, the journey was considerably easier, but the heat had been worse than either had expected, with sheltered areas few and far between. By the time they saw the cave's mouth, with trucks parked here and there nearby, they had both let out a cheer. They hurried over, both of them parched and exhausted. But it didn't take them long to realize something was very wrong. No one came out to greet them. When they stepped into the marginally cooler interior of the cave, the full truth hit them both smack in the face.

The cave had been the scene of a bloodbath.

The coppery scent of blood still hung in the air. Dark stains lay on the cave's floor and walls. The tables that had been set up to hold scientific equipment, laptops, and read-outs had been overturned, not one left standing. Crates of supplies and equipment had been demolished, the contents scattered far and wide.

Of the team of scientists Dr. Chalmers had assembled, very little was left.

Pliny let herself lean against the cavern wall, pressing her cheek to it and shaking silently. Dirk left her to her grief and did a cautious circuit of the cave. So far as he could tell, the team had been set upon very recently, perhaps as recently as the *Garuda* attack. The blood was still mostly fresh. The thing he liked least of all were the occasional footprints that showed up in the splashes of blood: broad, three-toed prints that suggested something reptilian. Reptilian, and very, very large.

*This is going to be ugly*, he thought. What the hell are the cops going to say? A tiny, weasely voice piped up inside him. *What do you think they're going to say? You know what the cops are like down here. You think they're going to buy some story about living dinosaurs? Or do you think they'll be more likely to pin the blame on the crazy Americans?*

An even more treacherous thought surfaced. Had Chalmers known about this all along? Had they been set up? But that didn't make sense. He had seen enough genuine grief since leaving his comparative easy life in the states to doubt Pliny's was real. Why would Chalmers put his granddaughter through something like this? Even if he were enough of a psycho to do just that, the presence of dinosaurs and pterosaurs and Pliny's magic stone lent a whole other dimension to the mess.

*It was enough to make a guy wish he hadn't gotten out of bed*, Dirk thought.

"Yes…all of them," a voice said behind him. He turned and saw Pliny talking on her phone—to Chalmers, he guessed.

"Grandfather, it's awful! I don't know what got them, but there's nothing left…"

He was content to let her debrief the old man for the moment. Right now, he wanted to get away from the carnage for a minute. If he could find something to drink, that would be even better. He couldn't remember the last time he'd been so thirsty.

One of the supply crates near the cave's entrance was filled with pre-packaged rations of dried meals and also bottled water. The water was warm—not to say hot—but Dirk downed a bottle without thinking about it. A second he emptied over his head, rubbing it into his face and onto his chest. He felt guilty for being so extravagant with the supplies, but the water cleared his head. He could actually think now.

Which was good, because they had to get the hell out of here. Where they would actually go, he had no idea, but this massacre hadn't started itself. Someone or something had done it, and they might be back for seconds at any time. Chalmers might already be summoning help for them, but Dirk had no intention of sitting and twiddling his thumbs until the old man got a helicopter out to them.

He strode out of the cave over to one of the trucks and checked the ignition. No key. Of course not. Chalmers' scientists had picked this of all moments to practice responsible car ownership. But there were two more trucks, and while he didn't like the idea of searching the remains in the cave, he would have to. He couldn't exactly ask Pliny to help out—she had probably known at least some of these people.

As he was turning from the truck, something very close by growled at him. The sound had a breathy overlay, as though it were being forced through flared nostrils. It didn't sound like a dog, or anything else he had ever heard growling. Just as the *Garuda*'s honking, screaming call had sounded completely unlike anything else.

*Aw, crap.* Dirk really didn't want to turn and look at the thing, but running blindly wasn't an option. The quick glance he allowed himself was more than enough.

The thing facing him on the other side of the truck was a big hairless quadruped, with a huge, heavily muzzled head and the same kind of pallid, somehow unhealthy-looking skin as the *Garuda*. Its flanks were striped with irregular bars of black. Dirk assumed it was a dinosaur of some kind (*just seems to be shaping up to be a dinosaur kinda summer*) but something about the shape of the thing's body and its stance—not to mention the stripes— reminded him more of a tiger. It was about the size of a tiger too, and as it sniffed at the air—sniffing *him*—its lips curled back from dagger-like, very capable-looking teeth. Its heavy muzzle was stained red in places. Dirk had no doubt he was staring down at least one of the creatures responsible for the slaughter in the cave.

Strangest of all were the flashing, multicolored jewels set into the skin around its thick neck. A sudden blast of memory took him back to the bus with Luis and Juan Pablo, listening to Juan Pablo's story of being attacked by vicious dogs wearing jeweled collars.

Suddenly, the story didn't sound so unlikely anymore, and Juan Pablo's "dogs," he suspected, weren't dogs at all. If only he'd known at the time. *Twenty-twenty hindsight, dude.*

Then suddenly Pliny's voice shrilled from inside the cave. "Dirk? Dirk, where are you? Grandfather says we have to get out of here right now!"

The younger Chalmers' voice made a very effective ice-breaker, so far as did the shriek she let out upon noticing the *Tigersaur*. The thing started violently, then rushed her, its clawed feet slapping on the stone.

Dirk acted without thinking, grabbing the first thing he saw in the truck's seat—a satisfyingly heavy tool-box—and flinging it underhand at the monster. The box bounced off the thing's head and clattered to the ground. The *Tigersaur*, clearly startled, snarled and turned its attention onto Dirk while a still-shrieking Pliny retreated back into the cave.

Dirk groaned inside. *No, no, not back there*! Unless he managed to run the *Tigersaur* off, sooner or later it would follow her in. And unless there was another entrance at the far end, she'd be trapped inside. His only hope would be to kill the thing before it had an opportunity to go after Pliny.

And at the moment, that seemed less than the likeliest outcome. The animal hauled itself onto the truck, trying to reach Dirk by the most direct route possible. Dirk jumped back and ran a few feet to the second truck. This one had a top, and he wasted no time scrambling in and locking the door.

The *Tigersaur* levered itself onto its hind legs, butting at the glass of the window with its head. Dirk hit the horn with his fist, but the blare only seemed to anger the creature. It slammed its head against the glass repeatedly. The window held, but Dirk knew it was only a matter of time before the thing broke in. He thought about opening the door on the other side and making a run for it, but he didn't like his chances; he had seen how quickly the thing ran.

That was when he noticed that whoever was in charge of *this* truck had blessedly left the key in the ignition. Dirk whooped with triumph when the engine turned over after one try. There wasn't much gas in the tank, but that didn't matter; he felt considerably better about his chances with a working vehicle between him and the *Tigersaur*. Even if he destroyed the vehicle in the process, the creature wouldn't find it easy to walk away after being rammed with a 2,000-pound truck.

But just as he put the truck in reverse, the *Tigersaur* moved its upper legs to the truck's hood and began hauling its huge body up onto the truck itself. The tires screamed against the stony ground, but the truck wasn't going anywhere; by then most of the *Tigersaur* was resting on the hood, its face giving Dirk an oddly insouciant look. Blasting the horn did no good at all.

Dirk's memory threw up a scene from some ancient comedy, probably one he'd watched with his grandmother, though it wasn't of the Bwana Don variety. In this movie, a man out for a Sunday drive had his way blocked on a country road by a lazy cow. The man—whom Dirk thought might have been W. C. Fields—yelled in inarticulate rage, leaning on his horn while the cow regarded him with regal disinterest. Fields' character had hardly been in danger of getting his face torn off, but beyond that, their situations were so similar Dirk had to restrain a burst of slightly hysterical laughter.

Something about the noises he was making seemed to displease the *Tigersaur*. In a single startled heartbeat, it went from bovine almost-slumber to a lashing, screaming juggernaut, clawing and head-butting the truck's windshield. Fine cracks spiderwebbed the glass; another butt turned the spiderwebs into an opaque white cloud. A third would demolish it entirely.

A loud *pop* sounded outside the truck, startling both Dirk and his attacker. Both turned their heads towards the cave and saw Pliny standing at the mouth, aiming a pistol at the *Tigersaur*.

"Pliny! Get out of here!" She must have found the pistol in the scattered supplies within the cave. Dirk could tell from her stance that she had shot before—her experience in that area surely outweighed his, but he also knew enough to realize the pistol wasn't going to do anything more than annoy the *Tigersaur*. It was already sliding its bulk off the truck's hood, its head trained on Pliny's small form.

"Go on!" Pliny cried, making shooing noises with one hand. If she was scared, Dirk couldn't detect it in her ferocious manner. "Get out of here. Leave him alone!"

The gun popped again. This time, whether by design or accident, the bullet found the *Tigersaur*. It spasmed violently in mid-stride, shrieking and seeming to bend in upon itself. Then it was tearing toward Pliny again. She feinted to the left, but the animal followed her motion and she was forced to flee to the cave's interior.

Meanwhile, Dirk was putting the truck in drive. A moment later, he was hot on the tracks of the monster. It was fast, but the truck was faster. The bumper caught it on the thing's flank, and it leapt aside, snarling—but then the front tires snagged its rear legs, pulling them under.

The sounds of bones breaking and the screaming of the animal as it thrashed in agony sickened Dirk, but now that he had an advantage, he couldn't let it get away. He hit accelerate, crushing its hind legs.

Pliny ran out of the cave, gun in hand. Dirk yelled and motioned for her to go back in, but she continued—though cautiously—until she was dangerously close to the *Tigersaur*'s snapping, foaming snout. Legs placed well apart, she lowered the barrel of the gun, took aim, and shot the creature squarely between the eyes. It jerked once and lay still.

Dirk let himself relax behind the wheel. "Thank God," he muttered. Then he caught sight of Pliny stroking the monster's head—almost tenderly, but also with a strangely distracted air, as though she were faced with a problem she couldn't quite solve.

"I don't know that that's such a good idea," he told her. Had he not felt on the verge of a nervous collapse, he would have been a little more forceful; who the hell knew what kind of unknown parasites or diseases something like this animal might carry?

"Something's strange," Pliny murmured finally, giving the thing a final stroke and standing up.

That was a little too much for Dirk. "Oh, you *think*? We were just attacked by a damned dinosaur, nearly eaten by it. You think something's a little off?"

"You know what this is, right?" Pliny said, pointing at the dead animal.

"What, that little gentleman right there? I'd say that's an unusually robust specimen of *biteyourassoffasaurus*."

"It's a gorgonopsian," Pliny said patiently. "I thought so at first, but now I'm sure of it. They weren't actually dinosaurs. They belonged to a completely different genus."

"Just like the rhampho-whatsis wasn't *actually* a dinosaur, according to your grand-dad? I mean, I gotta say, I'm a little disappointed. When are we going to get my face chewed off by an actual for-real dinosaur? Who do I talk to?"

He was aware that he was babbling, but Pliny didn't seem put off by it. She came up to the truck and leaned against it. "The point is that creatures like this actually predate what we think of as dinosaurs, even though in most ways they were more like mammals. That *Pteranodon* that attacked us…"

"Was *that* an actual dinosaur?"

"Well, no, it…*never mind*! The point is that that the fossils we have for that animal date from the Cretaceous Period, sixty-six million years ago. Gorgonopsians were from millions of years *before* that. And for that matter," she added thoughtfully, "they weren't native to South America. And for *that* matter, *Rhamphorhyncus* was a Jurassic animal. And most of *their* fossils were found in Europe."

"So?"

"*So*, what is a gorgonopsian doing flourishing in the same ecosystem as animals that only evolved millions of years after it had gone extinct…and which we know were from a completely different continent?"

"*We* evolved millions after the gorgon-whatsits too, Pliny. I'm a little more concerned with getting us out of this alive. I heard you talking to your grandfather back there. What did he say?"

"He…oh my God…"

Dirk knew damned well Chalmers had said no such thing. The sudden terror in Pliny's voice made him glance over his shoulder. A moment later, he was leaping over the truck's door, grabbing Pliny, and running for the cave.

# FIVE

What Dirk had seen in the brief moment he'd glanced over his shoulder was a pack of no fewer than five gorgonopsians stealthily approaching the truck. They had the same strangely pale, striped skin as their fallen brother, and the same glittering stones set into their skin. But they were, if anything, bigger. Much bigger. When Dirk's eyes connected with those of the lead animal, it and three of its friends switched from stalking to a flat-out run. The fifth elected to stay behind and refresh itself with the first gorgonopsian's corpse, tearing off huge mouthfuls of meat, which it swallowed whole with backward jerks of its head.

"Where'd you get the gun?" Dirk yelled, looking frantically around the cave's interior, hoping he'd missed something earlier that might help them now. Pliny jerked her head at a table and, standing her ground, took aim and began squeezing off rounds at the quartet of monsters. The gorgonopsians winced when they were hit, but the bullets seemingly did no more serious damage than a flock of mosquitos.

The table Pliny had indicated contained only a laptop, its screen blank. Whoever had been using this workspace had apparently set the pistol down just before they were attacked. Dirk saw no other guns in evidence, but there was a crowbar leaning against one of the crates. He snatched it up and ran back at the gorgonopsians boiling into the cave. His system was flooded with adrenaline; given a choice (and the ability), he would have teleported himself and Pliny to the nearest bar and ordered himself a very large bourbon. Any element of choice being lacking, he settled for shouting like a Neanderthal and meeting the gorgonopsians' attack head-on.

"The nose!" Pliny yelled. "Whack them on the nose!"

It sounded almost nonsensical, but Dirk had no objection to giving it a try. He lifted the crowbar and fetched the lead gorgonopsian a healthy wallop across the snout. The thing yelped and retreated a few feet, not seeming to understand what had just happened to it. By then, Dirk had distributed thumps to the other three, enough to hold them at bay, though apparently not enough to route them completely. If nothing else, they knew to treat the screaming lunatic with the iron bar with caution—otherwise, Dirk probably would have been dead.

"Dirk! Over here! Come on!"

Pliny's voice was behind him, at the rear of the cave. *She must have found a rear entrance*, Dirk thought, and turning, ran like hell, the sore-nosed gorgonopsians in hot pursuit.

The rear of the cave actually ended in a blank wall, but to the right was a passage that led deeper in. Pliny's voice continued to call to him from inside. The passage was narrow enough that the gorgonopsians couldn't follow in a group, and they didn't seem to have the intelligence to go through single file. They stood in a snarling, clawing mass, shoulders rubbing shoulders as each fought to break through and run their prey down. Dirk was happy to leave them behind.

After some uncomfortably close twists and turns, the passage opened up onto a vast chamber. This one looked different from the rough, uncut stone walls of the outer cave; the walls and ceilings here seemed smoother, as did the floor. More, there were what appeared to be designs cut into the stone—worn down long ago to almost nothing, but still just visible: regular geometric patterns and stylized figures that might have been attempts at depicting humans…or not. Something about the place felt more vital than the outer area; Dirk wasn't sure if it was the right way to put it, but it felt somehow more lived-in.

There were no tools or supplies scattered around that he could see. Dirk would have been surprised had Chalmers' team not discovered it. He was more interested in the fact that there was no hint of a back entrance to the cave. Instead, there was a sort of alcove set into the rear wall, large enough to hold several people standing upright. Pliny was inside it, running her hands over the faint carvings on the inner walls.

"What is this place?" Dirk asked. "And what's that thing?" He wanted to add, *Are you sure standing in it is a good idea*? He was exhausted and nervous. The sounds of the gorgonopsians snarling and scrabbling a comparatively short distance away didn't help. Neither did the fact that without the hoped-for rear entrance, they were effectively trapped. The animals weren't going to remain stuck forever. Even if Chalmers were sending a rescue party at that moment, there was a very real danger they could be slaughtered in a matter of moments.

Pliny seemed less worried. She was examining the carvings with loving care, tracing each in turn with a slow finger. "When I would ask what something was," she murmured, "Grandfather would always ask, 'What does it *look* like?'"

*Good old Grand-pap*, Dirk thought sourly. *What a genius.* "Well, *it looks like* an elevator," Dirk said irritably. "Kind of. But obviously it's not."

"Really?" Pliny turned and gave him a strange smile. "Come in here," she said. "Look at this."

Dirk stepped into the alcove beside her, keeping a tight grip on his crowbar. Pliny was standing on her toes, pointing at a depression in the upper wall. It was round, encircled by shallower oval hollows around a much deeper central depression. The whole thing looked a bit like a highly stylized sunburst. When Dirk looked more closely, he thought he could see something glassy shining inside the central hollow.

Dirk had no idea what he was looking at, or why Pliny seemed so fixated on it. She had thrust a hand under her collar and pulled out a pendant. It was disc-shaped with a lump of crystal set in the middle. It took Dirk a moment to catch the irregular way the stone flashed, as though with some kind of internal energy. It was, he realized, the same kind of stone Pliny had used to take down the *Rhamphorhyncus* back at the hotel, just smaller.

"Here," she said, removing the pendant from her neck. "Give me a hand."

"You want to—what? Put it in that hole?" For some reason, Kirk didn't like the idea of doing that. For that matter, he wasn't crazy about just touching it.

"Grandfather told me to. Just trust me…"

Loud scrabbling noises sounded from the passageway. A moment later, they were much louder. Somehow the gorgonopsians had managed to navigate the opening. Now one was rushing through, its flanks bloodied and its eyes murderous.

"We got company," Dirk said. *This is it*, he thought, tightening his grip on the crowbar. They weren't getting out of this. Even assuming Pliny got in a lucky shot with her pistol, or he managed to conk one of the things unconscious, there would be others right on its heels. They weren't going to survive. The monsters were coming, and there was nowhere to run.

"Do it!" Pliny screamed, jumping and slapping at his hand. "Do it, put it in! Hurry!"

Dirk did as she said, because, why not? Indulge the crazy girl before she was ripped into pieces. He slapped the pendant onto the depression in the wall and was a little surprised at the result. First, the pendant fit perfectly, its shape matching that of the hollows with surprising accuracy. Then there was a grinding noise, somewhere from deep in the earth—*no*, Dirk thought, *not just from below*; it was all around them, shaking the alcove as though determined to reshape it at the molecular level. Pliny grabbed his arm, whooping and hopping up and down as though she had just won a prize at the county fair.

"It's working! It's *working*! He was right!"

Outside, the other three gorgonopsians had burst into the chamber as well, but the tremors apparently unsettled them—much more than Dirk would have expected. They stopped in their tracks, lowering their heads, glancing nervously around as though wondering how in the hell they had found themselves in such a strange place. Eating humans suddenly seemed very low on their list of priorities.

A vast slab of stone began sliding slowly from right to left, cutting off the entrance of the alcove. Dirk yelped and grabbed at the stone's edge, but there was no holding it back—whatever force was moving it was remarkably powerful, and had Dirk not taken his hands away, they would have been crushed as the slab's edge slammed home. Pliny was shouting something he couldn't hear over the grinding of stone. She seized his arm to get his attention.

"I said hold on! It's going to be a long drop!"

"What do you mean a long—?" But that was all Dirk got out before the now sealed-off chamber began falling downward, at a steadily increasing speed that quickly became unbearable. Both were quickly forced to their knees. Pliny laughed and whooped, pumping a fist in the air while holding onto the floor with her free hand. Dirk screamed something that might have been a prayer, or equally well, a curse.

They were going somewhere. *Where*, he had no idea. Maybe there would be a place where gorgonopsians and pterosaurs were still extinct.

A guy could hope.

***

There was, Theophilus Chalmers reflected, something to be said for having the people who slaughtered and abducted your employees on speed-dial. If nothing else, it certainly saved time filling out police reports. As his smartphone shrilled away in his ear, he tapped impatiently on the scarred blotter covering the hotel room's desk. When the phone eventually kicked into voicemail, he angrily hit the END button and redialed.

While he waited, the old man cast a sour eye around his room. This was far and away the best accommodation the Grande could offer, but the furniture was still cheap and not at all in the best shape, the art on the walls garish and poorly-framed. Yet the hotel's owner had presented the room to him with hushed reverence, as though it were a suite fit for royalty.

Chalmers didn't look down on the citizens of Tacaraguita for their pretensions. After all, he had stayed in actual royal suites, and in his eyes, the multi-billionaires and petty nobility strutting about such places were far more contemptible. Really, who would give a second thought to king-sized beds and state-of-the-art *bidets* when an entire alternate civilization existed just beneath their feet? A civilization that completely contradicted their ideas of history and even evolution? Who could be that small-minded?

People were funny.

Finally, the ringing ended and a hoarse voice on the line grunted something—nothing so pleasant as a hello, of course.

"I have just spoken to my granddaughter," Chalmers said sternly. "What the hell are you people playing at?" He was not speaking English or Spanish—anyone eavesdropping on the call would have likely been mystified by the language he used, which was alternately sibilant and guttural. A linguist might have picked up some structural similarities to ancient Sanskrit, but it would be highly unlikely they could have even attempted a translation.

The hoarse voice did not reply.

"She tells me you attacked her and her party while they made their way to the cavern. I'm to understand you either killed Dr. Chandrasekaran or caused him significant injury. Would you care to explain yourself?"

More silence. Chalmers didn't expect a reply, but something in the silence irritated him profoundly.

"My granddaughter also tells me that they found the cavern empty and awash in blood. Then they were attacked by a hunting pack of *Marlgrym*. It's not enough that you tried to abduct her last night—under my very nose! You took it upon yourselves to mount a second attack upon my people…"

"The Lords, sair…their orders…"

Chalmers gritted his teeth. "Damn your Lords to their ancestors' lowest and hottest hell. Where is my granddaughter? Where is she *right now*?"

In fact, he had a fairly good idea where Pliny was. She had called from the cavern to report her situation and that had allowed Chalmers to tell her where to find the nearest escape route. He hadn't wanted to do that—he would have much preferred to keep up the wide-eyed charade of knowing nothing about the cavern, or what lay countless miles beneath it. But his hand had been forced. In any case, Pliny had been too panicked to do anything but obey him, and too intelligent to do anything else.

She was in all likelihood safe from Hrund's people. So was young Mr. Bannerman, which pleased Chalmers. At least now he didn't have to think of some excuse to keep Dirk with their party.

Still, what awaited the young people was impossible to predict.

"We do not know, sair. We did not find her…"

It was the answer Chalmers had expected—he certainly hadn't expected the idiot to confess that they'd sent *Marlgrym* into the cavern to run Pliny down. Even so, he gripped the phone so tightly he half-expected it to crack in his fist. "Damn you, we had an agreement!"

"We serve the Lords, sair," the voice said suddenly. "And the Lords only." There was a peevishness there Chalmers might have found amusing under other circumstances. Interesting how the sulkiness of a functionary being dressed down by a superior sounded much the same in any language. But there was a certain insolence in the voice as well, that of a peon semi-secure in the knowledge his *real* bosses would support him, no matter how many threats came at him from other quarters.

"Yes, you serve the Lords and the Lords' desires trump all others. I'm not so important, eh? Well, you listen to me, my friend…" Chalmers leaned forward in his desk chair, letting his rage build and focus. He disliked having to do this, especially considering the person he was speaking to ranked comparatively low in the *daitya* hierarchy. He would have much preferred to speak to one of their leaders—or still better, one of the "Lords" themselves. But they weren't likely to waste time justifying themselves to the likes of him.

It was time to "bring the shock and the awe," as Pliny would have gleefully put it.

"I am responsible for these people your little gang have so casually taken. Dr. Chandrasekaran is not merely an employee, he is a valued colleague. That goes for every one of the men and women you found in the cavern as well. Particularly Dr. Dvorak," he added. Anya…God only knew what *she* was making of all this…

"As for my granddaughter, I shouldn't need to tell you how important *she* is to me. I am coming now. You may tell your precious Lords that if I find you have so much as dislodged a hangnail on her little finger, I will make them pay for it."

Chalmers thought he could sense an intense nervousness seeping through the smartphone. Not surprising. This poor fool had some experience of the upper world, but he had no sure way of knowing what Chalmers could or could not do.

"You think this little speaking-device is all I bring to your world? Do you? Let me tell you, my friend…in my world, these devices, which are as high above your Lords' *mani* stones as a *mani* stone is above a *yaksha*'s hunting spear, are sold in the lowest markets as an amusement for children…" Which was an out and out lie, of course. Even a damaged *mani* contained immeasurably more power than the throwaway phone he'd bought and presented to Hrund's people as a means of "keeping in touch." But now that he'd told *one* lie…

"I have devices that could cause devastating storms in the earth, or bring terrible plagues to all your world's peoples. All the *yaksha*, all the *daitya*, and each and every one of your Lords. Your pasty little skins will bubble up and rot and fall off your bones. Is that what you want? *Is it?*"

Chalmers could hear the man briefly lose his grip on the phone, juggling it in agitation. "No, sair," he mumbled.

"No, you most assuredly do *not*. I will be at your camp in short order to straighten this out," Chalmers snapped, glaring at a still-life of a pot of marigolds. "Tell Hrund. Tell your Lords. Pray that I am not displeased by what I find."

With that, Chalmers ended the connection and leaned back in his chair. He had to move, to go *now*, but he was so damned tired. Just getting down here had expended so much energy and resources. He had called in every favor he was likely to get from everyone he knew.

What they were doing was necessary. He was convinced of that. Necessary and long overdue. But he was taking terrible chances. And all it would take was one misstep to bring it all crashing down around his ears.

\*\*\*

Hari Chandrasekaran was dreaming he was six years old again, sitting with his grandmother on the steps outside their home in Finsbury Park. He was wearing short pants and sandals, clutching a plastic tyrannosaur that even in his dream he knew was woefully inaccurate in terms of its anatomy. His grandmother was white-haired, with a querulous, wrinkled face like a walnut. She always wore a brightly colored *sari* and could not walk well without her cane, which she was now using to point out an ant creeping laboriously over the sidewalk.

"There, you see, Hari? You see that little ant?" Grandmother spoke Hindi; she had more or less refused to learn English since Hari's father had brought her to London. The move had not been easy on the old lady. She had never really approved of Hari's mother, who worked as a nurse at a local clinic. Since her arrival in England, she had spent most of her time in the room her son had carefully set aside for her.

Hari's father was a good man and had been deeply grieved at his mother's unwillingness to engage with her new world. He was not particularly religious, but now he offered prayer after prayer to Ganesha, the elephant-headed Hindu deity known as the Remover of Obstacles.

It took quite some time, but in the end, Lord Ganesha must have heard Sanjay Chandrasekaran's prayers. One night, Sanjay came home to find his mother busily cooking a curry, chatting happily with his wife, who joyfully told him she was pregnant with the child they had all longed for. From that day on, Sanjay's mother had lived for her grandson.

"You see how the ant is climbing into its hole, Hari?"

"That's where it lives," Hari said, a little primly. "The ants have a queen, just as we do." He had also benefited from Ganesha's role as patron of science and knowledge; he already showed the makings of the scientist he would one day become, and he had already easily mastered both English and Hindi.

"Yes, but if you could make yourself as small as that ant, and follow it down into its anthill, you would find more than just its home. If you kept following the tunnels, you would go deep and deep into the earth. The tunnels would grow wider and wider, and bright with light. Finally, they would lead you to Patala."

This was a story Hari had heard many times, and though he preferred books on science and animals to fairy tales, his grandmother's stories were sacred to him. "What is Patala, *Nani*?"

The old lady's eyes gleamed. "A great palace under the earth, where the *Naga*s and *Nagina*s live."

Hari knew that Patala was even more than that. And in this dream, he somehow knew that one day the influence of his *Nani*'s stories would lead him to embroider his scientific studies with world mythology and eastern occult traditions. One day, the scientist he would become would stumble upon a paperback book in used bookstall with the title *Patala: Lost World of the Serpent Kings* by one Theophilus Chalmers. He would seek out Dr. Chalmers and in time become his trusted assistant. But that would happen a long time from now. Today, he could listen to *Nani*'s stories, and then go listen to a football match with his father (perhaps Lord Ganesha was also a fervid Arsenal supporter) and then eat his grandmother's curry for dinner before welcoming his mother home from work. Life was simple now, and good.

"I wish I could see Patala," he said, with comfortable laziness.

"One day you will, when you are all grown up," *Nani* said, nodding as confidently as if she were talking about a trip by tube. "You will see amazing things. Things few other people have ever seen.

"But Hari, listen to me." His grandmother touched his hand, her old face gone hard and serious. "The *Naga*s do good in the world, but they can also be very wicked. So can the men who serve them. So when you do go to Patala, you must be very clever, and very strong."

"I will, *Nani*." The old lady's serious expression frightened him a little. It suggested life might not always be so simple or pleasant.

The dream ended abruptly. Suddenly, thirty years were added to his age, and he was not feeling at all well. Wherever he was, it was nowhere near London.

He was lying on his side on a rocky, barren landscape that seemed composed on every side of mountaintops. From the position of the sun overhead, he guessed it was late afternoon. He was hot and bruised and aching; he didn't suspect broken bones or any serious injuries, but every movement was answered by a sudden bolt of pain. The only good thing about his situation was that he was lying on a large sheet or tarpaulin of tanned leather. It wasn't much, but it was thick enough to prevent the stones underneath from digging into his side.

The place, wherever it was, was clearly a camp of some kind. Several fires were burning within circles of rocks, and the air was pungent with the smell of roasting meat. Men sat in small groups on all sides. Most wore simple kilts and sandals of tanned leather, with what Hari took to be machetes or short swords of black metal or stone. They were nasty-looking customers, heavily built, but with pale, sickly complexions. Glittering *mani* stones were set into their skin.

A number of large animals were lounging around the camp as well, creatures that resembled gigantic crocodilians more than anything else, but with an unmistakably mammalian cast to their bodies. Their skins were smooth, with the same pallor and irregular studding of colored stones. Hari guessed they were some species of gorgonopsians, viciously efficient predators whose bodies suggested mammalian predators who would evolve long after the theropod dinosaurs who succeeded them.

Towering over the party in the background was the *Pteranodon* that had earlier attacked his party. A gigantic azhdarchid, whose survival Chalmers had speculated on in his book, naming it for the giant flying *Garuda* of Hindu myth, sat prodding at its body with its huge beak. Grooming itself for parasites, Hari guessed. *Or maybe just diddling its bollocks. What the hell do I know?* He had studied creatures like these over his entire career, hoping against hope that his mentor's theories would prove correct and that he would have the opportunity to see them in the flesh. But now that he had that opportunity, he felt overwhelmed. Part of him wanted to walk over to the gorgonopsians and study every inch of them; another surprisingly large part wanted to simply run from them until he collapsed from exhaustion.

Still, this was an amazing opportunity, one he couldn't afford to pass by. The big *mani* stone he'd taken from Pliny was gone, as was all his gear except for the clothes he wore. By some miracle, he still had his phone, wedged deeply into his pocket, but he had no idea if he could get any reception out here—wherever "here" was—and taking it out would be nothing but an invitation to his captors to take it away. If he was going to record any of this, he was going to have to rely on memory.

He noticed a man walking directly toward him. The fellow was one of the pasty-skinned types seated around the cookfires, but he was wearing a sharp black suit and necktie, closer to East London gangster chic than the Neolithic garb of his companions. Hari thought about the men Chalmers had cautioned him about at the hotel—he certainly *looked* like one of them. And when Hari saw the small, greyish-white pterosaur clinging to his shoulder like a *panto* pirate's parrot, he knew for certain. Hari wondered how the man managed to maneuver around the stones in those flash leather brogues.

"You are up," the man observed, smiling in a not quite malevolent way. His accent put Hari in mind of Urdu and Slavic, yet was not quite like either. "I was worried Treszek might have hurt you more than necessary."

"Got a hard head," Hari told him, returning the smile, though with less confidence than he'd hoped. He thought Treszek was probably the *Garuda*. He actually hoped so. The other possibility was that "Treszek" was one of the other pale men, and he'd been knocking Hari around while he was unconscious.

"Don't suppose there's a chance of some breakfast?" Hari smiled. "I'd kill for an old bacon sarny and a cuppa." Actually, his stomach was feeling distinctly queasy, but if his guess was correct, he had been out most of the day, which meant he hadn't eaten in quite a while. He needed his strength, and since his guests seemed to be cooking, he saw no point in standing on ceremony.

"I'll see what can be arranged." The man unwound the little pterosaur from around his neck and tossed it into the breeze. A moment later, it was flapping toward the cookfires. The man sank down into a cross-legged position next to Hari, digging briefly in the inner pocket of his jacket.

"This is yours, I believe." He held out Hari's dog-eared copy of Chalmers' *Patala*, the book he had been reading before the *Garuda* attack. "I attempted to study it, but with little success. Your English is a strange language."

"Not the first time I heard that," Hari said, gratefully taking the book back. "You seem to be doing alright in the spoken word department," he observed.

"Yes. I speak several of your upworld languages. Basque I found much easier. I am called Hrund," he added. "Your own name I already know, Dr. Chandrasekaran."

The two sat staring at each other for a while, an echo of every uncomfortable silence at every faculty wine-and-cheese soiree Hari had ever attended.

"So, can we cut to the chase, as we upworlders say?" Hari asked finally. "Am I your prisoner, or what's the story?"

Hrund nodded. "For the moment, that is accurate. Your final fate will be decided once the Old Man joins us."

"The Old Man, eh? And who might that be?"

"At times, a friend to our order," Hrund said. "And sometimes an adversary, in truth. He is displeased that we have taken you."

"Your order?" He wanted to ask why the "Old Man" would be upset at his being a prisoner, but he decided to take things slowly.

"We are the Banished," Hrund said, as though this explained everything. "We no longer live among the true peoples below. Our race is the *daitya*, but we do seldom use that name among ourselves. It is our place to guard Patala—the world beneath— against upworlders."

Had Hari not been in such pain, he might have had to restrain himself jumping to his feet and punching air with a whoop of triumph. The names Hrund used—Patala, *daitya*—were the same as those used by Chalmers in his book. He had cribbed them from old Vedic writings, assigning them seemingly at random to the creatures and beings he felt sure inhabited the inner world.

*Be careful, Hari*, a voice said in his head. An old woman's voice, startlingly like his *Nani*'s. *Why would this strange man be using the same names old Theo did, when Theo just plucked them from the air? He could just as easily have told you he belonged to the sacred tribe of Flopsy, Mopsy, and Cottontail.*

The voice continued. *Besides, he just gave you old Theo's book, didn't he? He could have pulled those names directly out of it to manipulate you. Don't be so eager to eat out of his hands.*

Hari calmed himself with a certain amount of effort.

"Had much trouble with us upworlders, have you?" he said, clearing his throat.

"They come occasionally," Hrund said. He loosened his tie, his pallid, meaty fingers much nimbler than Hari would have expected. "They have no true knowledge of Patala, but they have stories of it. They believe it to be a place of great riches and marvels. So they come, searching for our filthiest herd animals— our *grym*. 'Dinosaurs,' they call them. Others of your race are more enlightened. They search for these."

He pulled the collar of his shirt down, revealing an irregular row of gems that looked as though they'd been pressed into his skin like stones into warm wax. "The *mani*," he said solemnly. "Slavery to us, yet to the Lords—and your people—power unimaginable."

*Oh yes*, Hari thought, keeping his face solemn. *I've seen those before*. The stones were Chalmers' best proof that his theories were correct. He had been very careful with them, keeping them from everyone except his most trusted associates.

A loud flapping sounded nearby. The *Rhamphorhyncus* was back, a leather sack gripped in its lower claws. It dropped the sack between the two men.

Hrund blinked placidly. "As I believe your people say, 'lunch is served.'" If there was an ounce of real humor in his voice, Hari couldn't detect it. He opened the bag and found a disc of leathery, unleavened bread, a smaller leather flagon that he was happy to find contain tepid but reasonably fresh water, and a large chunk of flesh that had been not so much cooked as charred evenly on all sides.

The meat was oily and strong-smelling, but when accompanied with a bite of bread and chased with a healthy swig of water, it could be kept down. He had no particular interest in asking Hrund what animal the meat had come from.

"I don't suppose it'd do any good to tell you my friends and I are just scientists…seekers of knowledge."

"That is for the Old Man to judge," Hrund said. "As I said, he will join us in due course. In the meantime, there is much we can discuss."

"Oh, really?" Hari asked, chewing the meat as completely as he could. It was already coming back on him with strong, fishy-tasting burps.

"Yes. Among our order, I am considered favored. I have walked in your world's cities, tasted your culture. It is degenerate, sickeningly so, and yet…"

"And yet?" Hari watched him carefully.

"There were elements I found…extremely interesting. I have longed for an upworlder of your education to discuss them with."

He could see signs of some volcanic passion simmering under the man's calm demeanor, seeking expression. *Please tell me you weren't hanging out at the Roxy back when Sid and Johnny used to play…right now, I think I could take anything but a closet punk fan.*

"Dr. Chandrasekaran," Hrund said, leaning forward with the unmistakable gleam of the zealot in his eyes. "Have you ever been to the *theater*?"

# SIX

As soon as Dirk woke, he wanted—desperately—to fall asleep again. He felt as though he had been flattened under an enormous rolling pin, all the vitality methodically crushed out of him and replaced with something excruciatingly painful—broken glass, perhaps.

Still, he was alive. That was something. And he was no longer falling at breakneck speed, which was a definite plus. The very fact that his bones hadn't shattered into jelly upon impact was enough for him.

But where the hell was Pliny?

The sheet of stone that had blocked the doorway had retracted again. Outside was jungle, humid but not oppressively so. Lush greenery was everywhere, a crazy mixture of waist-high plants and towering barrel-trunked trees topped with vast, fernlike leaves. Someone had waded out into the green, leaving a trail of bent and broken stems that was already starting to close in on itself. It had to have been Pliny.

Wincing a little, Dirk stepped outside. The "elevator" that had delivered them to this place was no longer part of a wall; on this end, it opened out from a stone pillar that rose from the ground like an umbilicus, connecting what looked like miles above to a layer of misty clouds. In the places where the clouds were partially dispersed, Dirk saw not blue sky but what looked like roughly textured stone, like the roof of a cave.

There was light, with the bright intensity of a spring morning. The source of it was a vast, blazing sphere that hung over the landscape. It was too bright to look at directly, but Dirk knew it wasn't the sun—at least, not the sun he knew. The air was fragrant with vegetation—not particularly fresh, but that was only to be expected in a jungle, he supposed.

Dirk cleared his throat. "Pliny?" he said, then repeated it, louder. He was a little worried about what his voice might attract, but when there was no answer, he went back into the elevator, picked up his crowbar (impossible not to think of it as "his" now), and set out to follow Pliny's trail. He still felt responsible for her; there was no telling what she might run into in this place.

Besides, she had the amulet or talisman or whatever it was that had brought them to this place—and at least in theory could take them back. He wasn't particularly interested in going back to tango with the gorgonopsians, but he certainly didn't intend to take up permanent residence in Jungle World.

As he moved further away from the elevator, the ground rose slightly, and the vegetation covering it diminished in height from waist to ankle level. As Dirk crested the lip of the low hill, he was confronted by what he first thought were a herd of cows. They moved slowly, munching placidly on the plants, occasionally pausing to enjoy an explosive bowel movement.

Except the cows he was familiar with weren't olive green, with horned, bony shields incorporated into their faces. *Holy crap*, he thought. *Are those* Triceratops? These creatures didn't have the vicious, lance-like horns he remembered from his childhood reading—their horns were far shorter and more blunt-looking— but overall, they looked more like *Triceratops* than anything else he could think of.

He picked his way through the herd with downcast eyes, the better to avoid fresh patties of dino-dung. Suddenly, he heard a familiar voice cooing in the distance, and when he lifted his head, there was Pliny, seated cross-legged before one of the animals, feeding it a freshly plucked bouquet of greenery. The animal was far too large to be called a baby, but it was smaller than the others, and it moved a bit more quickly than its elders. Pliny teased it with the vegetation, tickling its beaked mouth before surrendering the food. It honked querulously, but seemed to prefer being fed to tearing up the food on its own.

"You sure that's such a good idea?" Dirk asked, moving cautiously toward her. The bigger animals paid him no attention at all, but if they got it in their heads to do a little trampling, he wanted to be ready to run.

Pliny beamed. "Look at them! Do you *see* them?"

"Yeah, I see them," Dirk said. "They're awesome. But shouldn't we be finding a way out of this place instead of playing Jurassic Petting Zoo?"

"Oh, you're hopeless!" Pliny relinquished her handful of plants and kissed the baby *Triceratops* on the nose before getting up to face him. "Don't you get it? These animals aren't just tame. They've been domesticated! Look!"

She pointed at a particularly large specimen ambling past. At first, Dirk didn't see what she meant; then he saw the leather straps fastened around the animal's midsection. On top was something like a modified saddle.

"It would have taken generations to tame a population of dinosaurs—even herbivores! That means there are people here, just like Grandfather thought!"

"Oh, so *these* are full-fledged dinosaurs," Dirk said, looking distrustfully down at the baby, which was eyeing his boots with some appetite.

"I can't figure out what species they are," Pliny said. "They're either relatives of *Triceratops* or they were bred from them. But down here, we might encounter all kinds of completely unique species, unknown in the fossil record."

"Yeah, about that," Dirk said. "Where *are* we, exactly?"

Pliny gave him an exasperated look. "This is the inner world my grandfather told you about just the other night. Patala! And it's a reality, just as he described in his book! Oh, I always believed in it, of course, but to actually *be* here…!"

Dirk glared. "If you burst into song right now, I'm going to paste you one. And what was the deal with that elevator-thingy? You're saying it was built by the people down here?"

"It must have been. If my grandfather is right—and it certainly seems he was—this entire environment was constructed millennia ago, as a refuge for advanced races. They must have needed occasional access to the upper world."

"Constructed…including the sun?" Dirk asked, nodding at the gleaming light in the sky. How exactly did you "construct" a sun?

"Including the sun," Pliny said, nodding. "Of course, it's not a sun in the same sense ours is. It's more likely an enormous *mani* stone, like the one I used to call off the *Rhamphorhyncus*. The stones are what power the entire civilization. I can't imagine how they got it into the sky, though." She shook her head dreamily. "They must be truly amazing people."

"Yeah. What do they do for when it's time to power down and get some Zs?"

"They don't. Unless there's some mechanism that allows the sun-stone to periodically darken or 'set.'"

*Is that why it's so green down here?* Dirk wondered. Maybe the stones gave off some kind of radiation that helped the plants grow. He felt no particular interest in giving Pliny the opportunity to speculate any more on this place. Time to start asking the hard questions.

"Well, anyway, now that we're down here, how do we get back *up*?"

Pliny goggled her eyes at him. "Are you kidding? This is the chance of a lifetime! Were you even listening to me? This is an artificial subterranean environment constructed by people who were flourishing when the rest of humanity had barely come down from the trees! There are living dinosaurs down here, and who knows what else! This will completely rewrite the history books! I'm not just talking about me or Grandfather. You'll be part of it as well. Your name will be in those history books, just like ours."

"Yeah, well, that's all above my paygrade. I agreed to get you to the site, and as far as I'm concerned, I've gone above and beyond that."

Pliny turned to face him, her fists clenched. Dirk was startled by how angry she looked.

"So what, then? You want to go home now? To what? To live in a poky little room in a nowhere town and be a laborer all your life? To be utterly insignificant? Fine, then. You go and do that."

With that, Pliny turned and stormed away across the green. Once, she jerked violently and cursed as she apparently stepped directly in a *Triceratops* pat. Moments later, she was a very small figure on the horizon.

Dirk watched her go, a stupefied expression on his face. This was the first time Pliny had exhibited anything like bad temper, and it was so intense that it left him without a response.

Only moments later, once Pliny's bobbing head had completely disappeared, did the anger come rushing back. "You hired me, damnit!" he shouted, knowing damned well she couldn't hear him. "I'm supposed to be your bodyguard! This place is dangerous! You think you're so self-sufficient, Miss Harvard graduate? You're not going to last five minutes without someone wiping your butt!"

After about half an hour of ranting to impassive dinos, he started walking again, in roughly the same direction Pliny had gone, the crowbar resting atop his shoulder. He was fuming, but most of the sting had gone. *Most* of it. He couldn't argue with most of what Pliny had said, which was really not much more (and considerably less) than his dad had been telling him since he hit puberty. He was a slacker, pure and simple, and he knew it. Had Old Man Chalmers handed him the money to start a real tour business, instead of babysitting his genius granddaughter, he would have hemmed and hawed and prevaricated and let the offer dry up untested. Given a magical opportunity to get back to the surface world right then, he would have gone straight back to his room and prayed that Marcus would take him back the next day. Because it was easier. Because the risk of failure was so much less.

But what the hell gave *her* the right to say that? Like she was his mother or his guidance counselor.

As he walked, he kept glancing over his shoulder at what he now thought of as the elevator tower. Even if he couldn't use it to get back up to the cavern, it was a comforting presence, and he wasn't likely to lose sight of it anytime soon.

At least, not until the grasslands gradually gave way to more of the stubby, barrel-shaped trees, which multiplied until he was walking through a forest. The land here was wet and muddy—not quite swampy, but close to it, enough to make walking uncomfortable. The further he moved into the forest, the more pools of standing water he saw. Dirk wondered if the trees' thick roots somehow worked to collect water and retain it. Their upper branches, with their fernlike leaves, blocked a lot of the sun-stone's light and heat. The area had a distinctly creepy look, and Dirk founding himself eyeing the pools with increasing nervousness. It was too easy to imagine a tentacle whiplashing out of one and wrapping itself around his ankle before dragging him to a watery death.

There was no sight or sound of Pliny, which made him still more nervous. *Where the hell had she gone? Had she angled off in a completely different direction at some point?* He didn't like that thought; if she had, it might mean he had lost her completely.

When he heard the scream, it was both a relief and a confirmation of even worse fears. He ran in the direction of the noise, bounding over stones protruding from the muck, doing everything he could to keep his ass going. He didn't like thinking about what he was going to find. A file marked PREHISTORIC MONSTERS flung itself open in his imagination and spat out any number of extremely unpleasant images, all scales and tusks and disemboweling claws. Pliny figured in all of these images, screaming piteously as whatever horror Dirk's mind chose to show him advanced on her.

What he actually found was almost worse, though it took him a moment to process it.

The muddy ground opened up onto a spreading depression, a couple of feet lower than where he stood. Pliny lay on her side, covered with mud. She had a hand pressed against her boot—Dirk guessed the depression had taken her by surprise and sent her tumbling, possibly hurting her ankle. It got worse, though. With her other hand—her left, and Dirk couldn't remember any evidence that she was ambidextrous—she was holding a long stick, poking it with savage intensity at something that reared up over her like a massive black cobra, hissing and trying to get in a strike.

It wasn't a cobra, though; in some ways, that was the worst part. A cobra would have been at least familiar. *This* was something that called to mind the worst parts of a scorpion, a spider, and a centipede, all tangled up together. It had to be a good eight feet long from its back end to its snapping, hissing mandibles. Pliny had so far managed to keep the thing from swarming on top of her by slashing at it as though her stick were a pirate's cutlass. Besides, the thing had more tactics at its disposal than just rearing and hissing. Every now and then, it spat what looked like a white mist at Pliny, which settled into a sticky, fibrous mass on her clothes and limbs.

*Like cobwebs*, Dirk thought blearily. They didn't look like much at the moment, but they were thickening fast. If it got enough of that crap on her, she wasn't going to be able to move. Then it would be game over.

"Hey!"

Dirk ran down the slope into the depression, barely managing to keep his balance as his boots skidded in the mud. Remembering his experience with the gorgonopsians, he fetched the centipede-thing a whack upside the head with the crowbar and it reared back, hissing violently. White webbing sprayed from its mandibles, coating the crowbar and most of Dirk's hand in the bargain. Dirk struck again before he realized he was making a serious mistake. When the crowbar struck the creature, the webbing stuck the iron to its exoskeleton—and Dirk's hand to the iron.

"Oh, God," Dirk groaned, yanking his arm back reflexively. All he succeeded in doing was hauling the centipede creature's head back with it. He wasn't able to break free from the webbing. He was able to keep the thing's clattering mandibles at arm's length, but sooner or later, it was going to get a bite in, or get its lower half wrapped around his legs and pull him down.

*How do I get myself into these things?* He thrust his arm downward, trying to pin the thing's head to the ground while he fixed a boot on top of it. The creature's instincts apparently told it that allowing itself to be subdued in this way was a bad idea; it hissed and thrashed violently from side to side, until Dirk was afraid that what would break was not the webbing, but his wrist.

Pliny, meanwhile, had apparently lost her mind. She had managed to get up and was leaping around Dirk and his attacker, beating at it with her stick. All the while she was shrieking "Help! Please, *help!*" Occasionally, she would thrust a thumb and forefinger between her lips and let rip with an ear-piercing whistle.

*Who the hell does she think she's calling?* Had Dirk been less busy trying to keep his limbs and face away from the centipede-creature's snapping jaws, he might have asked her directly.

Suddenly, there was a *whooshing* sound, and a wooden shaft materialized on the thing's black armor, protruding from a narrow space between two of its stomach-plates. The centipede shrieked and pulled itself up, nearly tearing Dirk's arm from its socket. Several more of the shafts popped up on its underside—not enough to bring it down, but enough, from the noise it was making, to cause it considerable pain.

Something came crashing up and over the slope, followed a moment later by another something that towered over it. It took Dirk a moment to realize that the first something was one of the *Triceratops*-like dinosaurs from the grasslands. The other was a dinosaur as well, but it was bipedal, a good seven feet high at the shoulder. It had cheetah-like spots on its back, black against a tawny gold-brown. Its overall build was sleek, the skin shining. It would have been an elegant-looking creature, had its upper limbs not been armed with sickle-like claws. It stalked forward with its head down, on a level with its outstretched tail, its serpent-like head intent on the hissing, snapping centipede.

Both dinosaurs wore leather saddle-harness combinations like the ones in the grasslands, allowing them to carry human riders. The biped's rider was a woman who looked as though she had stepped right out of a comic book. She had tousled bronze-colored hair and strong, angry-looking features. Her outfit was a sort of bikini of well-tanned leather, with greaves of the same material protecting her legs and lower arms. Her bare feet were hooked into stirrups built into her mount's harness. She carried a bow that she was even now pulling back, aimed at the centipede thing. An ululating cry broke from her throat.

The *Triceratops'* rider was also female, but she might have been from a completely different species of human. Dirk guessed she was a little older than Pliny, and much taller, her dark hair worn loose, with a crazy assortment of leaves and various detritus filling it. Her round spectacles seemed to magnify her huge brown eyes, which looked fearful but also determined. She wore the same kind of Bwana Don outfit as Pliny, but hers had seen better days and was missing the boots. Her long, mud-stained bare feet were positioned behind the *Triceratops'* head—a memory flashed back to Dirk of a TV show he'd seen about elephant riders in India, using their feet to guide their mounts. He guessed the girl had abandoned her boots for the same purpose. She slapped at the creature's sides with her open palm, urging it forward.

Dirk had only a moment to take all this in. The "cave girl" had loosed her arrow and was already nocking another. Dirk felt a whoosh of wind as the arrow hit the centipede's underside. It was trying instinctively to get down, hiding its vulnerable belly, but Dirk, both hands on his crowbar, managed to hold it upright.

That did it. Another hiss sounded as a fresh arrow buried itself in the underside of the creature's middle—about where Dirk guessed its vital organs might be. Sure enough, this time the hit was fatal. The thing went limp, its sudden weight dragging Dirk down with it as it fell.

As Dirk worked awkwardly to tear the crowbar free of the webbing that held it to the creature, he was vaguely aware of loud shrieks rising all around him. They weren't much like the cave girl's whooping battle-cry, but they were, if anything, even louder. Finally, he managed to get his hand loose and rose cautiously to his feet, half-expecting to feel another arrow slam into him at any second.

But the shrieks were not battle-cries. They came from Pliny and the tall *Triceratops* rider, who were bouncing up manically up and down, hands gripping each other's arms, squealing in what was evidently recognition and delight. The cave girl stood to one side, watching them with a bemused expression.

Meanwhile, the bipedal dinosaur picked its way over to the fallen centipede and sniffed at it. It then sniffed at Dirk, its nostrils dilating and snapping shut. Dirk took that as a sign it was a good time to join the girls.

"Dirk, this is Monica Jenkins! She's one of the scientists who was working at the site!"

"Oh, right. Good to hear you're not dead," Dirk said, shaking hands with the tall scientist. Her grip was disconcertingly strong, and she didn't immediately seem willing to release his hand. There was an odd little smile on Monica's face. Dirk had never seen himself as a terribly intuitive person, but something told him that Monica was finding the freedom of her new environment inspiring, maybe even a little intoxicating. He had a feeling the Monica Jenkins of the upper world was probably not so aggressively playful with men. He finally reclaimed his hand, but not without some effort.

"How'd you know to call for them?" he asked Pliny, who was still smiling adoringly at her friend.

"I saw Monica on the *Triceratops*, through the trees. Only I didn't know it was her at first, of course. I thought it was one of the people who'd domesticated the *Triceratops*..."

"*Horgrym*," Monica said gently. "They call them *horgrym*."

"Domesticated the *horgrym*," Pliny amended. "And the *horgrym* were so sweet, I knew they had to be friendly. So I just shouted out for help and…oh! Ohmigod, is Anya okay? I didn't even ask you. What about Lenny?"

Monica beamed. "They're all okay. Paul, too." When Pliny gave her a lost expression, she said, "You probably don't know him. He's our geologist."

"Oh God, Monnie, we thought you were all dead! We thought you and the others were…" Pliny's voice trailed off. She looked like she was moving quickly from relief to a kind of shock. "When we got to the cavern, there was blood everywhere! "

"Really? Those pale men must have done that after they put us in the elevator…or whatever it's called. Perhaps they wanted to scare off anyone else who happened on the cave. That would be my best guess, anyway. If I were them, I wouldn't want people coming down and opening up hamburger franchises and whatnot."

The cave girl, her interest in the conversation apparently at an end, stalked off toward the dead centipede. Dirk followed at a distance, content to leave Monica and Pliny to their reunion. Cave girl's raptor was sniffing at the centipede in an increasingly interested manner, but moved aside when its mistress seated herself beside it. Unsheathing a black-bladed knife, she sawed off one of the thing's smaller legs and flung it to the dino. It snapped the limb out of the air like a trained Doberman going for a biscuit. Then she plunged the blade into the centipede's underside, sawing energetically down the middle with a crispy sound that reminded Dirk of the crab dinners he and his family used to enjoy in southern Maryland when he was a kid.

"So what do they call you?" he asked. He wasn't exactly trying for a date, but he found the girl kind of fascinating. And if Dr. Monica Perkins could explore her aggressive side down here, he saw no reason he couldn't do the same thing. The woman gave him a quizzical look.

"Me Dirk," he said, touching his chest. Pointing at her, he asked, "You…?"

"Ah," the girl said, comprehension dawning on her face. Touching her own chest, she spat out a string of clashing syllables as long as Dirk's arm.

"Oh, that's Olga," Monica said suddenly, turning her attention to them. "That's what I call her anyway. She reminds me of a Russian *au pair* I had as a girl. Her real name is mostly untranslatable. It's a lot of 'daughter ofs' and 'wielder ofs' and 'rider ofs.' I don't think her people use names the same way we do."

"Okay," Dirk said, a little uncomfortably. Monica had sidled up next to him, standing so close that Dirk edged away slightly, in a purely reflexive motion. The tall woman, apparently not done with testing his limits, edged closer to him, smiling intently. Dirk tried to catch Pliny's eye, but she was engaged in loudly blowing her nose. She kept her head turned, but Dirk saw her smiling evilly to herself.

*I'll get you for this*, he thought, more in irritation than actual anger. He didn't exactly find Monica repulsive, but he wasn't used to a woman being so into him that she didn't even stop to blink. It was kind of unsettling.

"And what's *your* name?" Monica asked, not quite batting her eyes.

"Dirk," he said. "Dirk Bannerman. I'm, uh…Pliny's grandfather hired me. I was supposed to guide Pliny out to the cavern, but I guess I didn't do a very good job, or we wouldn't be down here." That thought reminded him of something that might just be an opportunity to change the subject.

"You were telling Pliny something about being taken prisoner by someone. You mean the big guys with the white skin?"

"Oh yes. It was odd because it wasn't exactly like them taking us prisoner. I mean, they weren't exactly friendly—they made it clear we had no choice—but we were just so fascinated by them. After all, they were part of the reason we'd come here. So we didn't even think about trying to escape. We just went right along with them, into the stone elevator…"

"How did they activate it?" Pliny asked, holding out her pendant. "Did they have *mani* stones, like this?"

"No," Monica said thoughtfully. "Instead, they seemed to use the smaller ones set into their skins. They just sort of flashed a few times and down we went. Then they more or less pushed us out and went back up. After some wandering around, we stumbled onto Olga's people not long after. They were very nice to us, luckily. They've sort of adopted us."

By now, Olga had finished slaughtering the centipede, dividing the carcass into slabs of whitish, fibrous meat and a small mountain of black shells. Working methodically, she began loading the meat and the better part of the shells onto the leather saddle-and-straps arrangement on the *horgrym*. Her raptor took care of the scraps and offal.

"You two can ride with me on Bossy here," Monica said, slapping the *horgrym*'s thigh. "There's not really any room on Olga's raptor, and he tends to move very quickly anyway."

"Where are we going?" Dirk asked. It took Monica a moment to answer; she seemed to be trying to impress with her mounting skills, but she nearly fell off twice.

"Why, back to Olga's village, of course. You two must be exhausted, and I'm sure you're both famished."

"Shouldn't we get back to the elevator?" Dirk asked. He was relieved to see Pliny climb up behind Monica, leaving the rear space for him...but the moment he climbed aboard "Bossy," Pliny slipped nimbly off and reseated herself behind him.

"Come on, push up," she said, poking at his ribs. "Don't be shy. Monica won't bite. Will you, Monica?"

"Not unless you beg me," Monica said, grinning slyly over her shoulder. Before Dirk could come up with a suitable reply—he was trying for something politely dismissive, but still as pleasingly roguish as he could manage—Bossy stood up and began stumping along at a fair pace, following the sprinting raptor out of the swamp.

*I hope I don't regret this*, Dirk thought unhappily.

# SEVEN

By the time Hrund paused to take a breath, the sun was low in the reddening sky. Hari had actually nodded off once or twice during the "conversation"—really more of a monologue. Hrund had sent his pet back for more water-skins, so he could soothe his throat as he went on about his favorite subject.

Hari had known one or two theater mavens during his time at Oxford. The worst ones were always from the provinces, drunk on the sudden feast of riches suddenly laid before them. But suburbanites and farm boys had nothing on Hrund of the Inner World, who had apparently stumbled into a Joe Orton festival some years before during a routine foray into London.

*Everything* about the theater fascinated him, from the smallest technical details of stagecraft and makeup to broad theories of acting. Apparently, he had originally thought that plays were some form of religious ceremony; he treated them with the same reverence.

"Anywhere I can use the facilities?" Hari asked, breaking abruptly into the *daitya*'s ecstatic chatter. Hrund stared at him, clearly with no idea what he meant.

"Loo? W.C.?" Hari rubbed his belly ruefully. "Hate to say it, but that lunch isn't sitting too well."

"Ah. Of course. We do not stand on ceremony here, Dr. Chandrasekaran. Behind that bush will do."

"You might not stand on ceremony, mate, but I do. I don't like to offend. Got anywhere more private?"

After some thought, Hrund pointed out another bush, somewhat further away.

"Please hurry back, Dr. Chandrasekaran. I'm anxious to tell you about the truly marvelous staging of Harold Pinter's *The Room* I saw at the Brighton Fringe Festival."

"And I'm anxious to hear about it," Hari said, flashing him a brilliant smile before hurrying off to the bush. He knew he didn't have a lot of time. Making an actual escape was probably not in the cards, not with gorgonopsians and pterosaurs ready to run him down at the first sign he was gone. But he still had his phone.

He crouched down behind the bush and took it out, hands shaking as he dialed Dr. Chalmers' number. A mechanical voice told him the call could not go through.

"Shit." Hari hadn't been so foolishly optimistic to believe he would get service out here—wherever *here* was. Still, they weren't completely in the hinterlands…were they?

It occurred to him he had no real idea where he was. He assumed he was still in South America, up in the mountains. But there was every possibility he had been flown via *Pteranodon* to somewhere far more remote. For all he knew, he might be on a mountaintop in China.

He tried the email app on his phone; nothing came up. He made another call to Chalmers' number. This time, the call seemed to go through, though the sound was hissing and indistinct.

"Dr. Chalmers," he said quickly. "It's me, Hari. Don't have much time." He opened his mouth to continue, then slowly closed it. What was he supposed to say, exactly? I've been kidnapped by the *daitya*, I'm on a mountain, they have vicious, meat-eating dinosaurs, please come quick? In the end, it didn't matter. The signal died before he could say another word.

If the call went through, even in incomplete form, Chalmers could surely trace it. But, even assuming he noticed it, it would take him a while, and by then, Hari could have been spirited off anywhere. The "Old Man" was coming, after all.

He rose from a squat to a crouch, glancing around. It wasn't quite night yet, and he could see the mountain before him sloped sharply downward. That was a good thing—in fact, it was fantastic. If he tore off running, inertia would lend him a certain amount of speed before his pursuers could catch up with him. And said pursuers likely wouldn't include the gorgonopsians—their long, low-slung bodies would have a hard time negotiating a steep incline; more likely they would go tumbling nose over tail right past him. Also, there might be cave entrances on the way down that he could hide in. The main thing was to get away from the *daitya*. He could then find his way to a town or village with cell phone service, and there reconnect with Chalmers. Before he had fully committed himself to escape, he had begun picking his way down the slope.

"Dr. Chandrasekaran!" It was Hrund's voice, not suspicious as yet, or angry, but definitely eager for his return. "Are you well? You haven't lost yourself, have you?"

The danger of discovery drove Hari to move more quickly, until he was leaping from place to place on the slope like a goat. He heard shouting behind him—none of it in English—and the hissing sound of stones sliding down the slope in miniature avalanches.

Something small zipped past his head—the *Rhamphorhyncus*. The little monster screeched as it orbited his head, making periodic dives. At a conference once in the Pacific Northwest, Hari had made the unwise choice of walking in a forest where crows were nesting. The birds were smaller than English ravens, but they weren't lacking in fighting spirit. Mama and Papa Crow had launched a full-out attack on him, diving and swooping as he ran for cover. At first, he had thought it almost funny—until he realized they were trying for his eyes.

Hrund's pet was every bit as vicious as the crows—and faster, to boot. Hari couldn't get away from it, and shielding his eyes made it difficult to see where he was going. Finally, his foot hit a protruding root and he went down hard. Suddenly, he was rolling down the slope, much as he had earlier imagined the gorgonopsians doing. Stones tore at his clothes and skin and battered at his limbs and head. When he finally came to a halt, stopped by a ledge a bit too large to roll past, he was a bloody, aching wreck.

Getting up was the last thing he wanted to do, but he knew he couldn't afford to rest. But when he clambered unsteadily to his feet, his old friend the *Rhamphorhyncus* was back, squealing and zipping round his head again. When Hari risked a look behind him, he saw several of Hrund's friends skidding down the mountainside. They hadn't brought gorgonopsians with them, and each held an unsheathed machete that looked every bit as dangerous as the monsters' fangs.

Hari turned to look over the ledge. The rest of the way down the mountain was considerably steeper. Making a run for it would almost certainly result in another fall, and that would almost certainly result in broken bones.

"Alright," he croaked, holding up his hands. "White flag. I surrender, yeah?"

The first of the *daitya* pointed back to the slope with his machete, snarling.

Hari swallowed. "Alright. Okay. I'm coming."

The men weren't gentle with him as he made his way back up the slope. Several times, he got slapped with the flat of a machete. He guessed the *daitya* took his attempted escape as a personal affront. Maybe Hrund had given them hell about it.

In fact, when they made it back to the camp, Hrund did not look at all pleased. His slab-like features glowered. "I am disappointed, Dr. Chandrasekaran. I thought you and I had a certain rapport."

"Oh, come on," Hari said, trying for a smile. "You can't blame a fella for trying, now can you?"

Hrund shook his head. "It is fortunate for you that we need you. Otherwise, we would not be so lenient. Also, the Old Man is here. He would have a word with you."

"The old fella, eh?" A faint spark of hope kindled inside Hari. He had no idea what kind of person the Old Man might be, but if the likes of Hrund had brains enough to relish a well-staged regency farce, there was surely hope this elder figure might have enough intelligence to be reasoned with.

"Alright. Take me to him. Your leader. Your…wait, you've never heard that? Come on, you've seen *Loot* six times, but you've never heard 'take me to your leader…'"

Hari's blustering was interrupted by a tall figure striding out of the shadows, his appearance breaking off Hari in mid-sentence. The "Old Man" was a man, right enough, and definitely old; an old white man in khakis, jodhpurs, and boots, his face half-hidden by a huge, bristling white mustache. Hari recognized him immediately.

"Dr. Chandrasekaran, I presume," Chalmers said, smiling apologetically. "I'm sorry our reunion had to take place under these circumstances. You're alright? No broken bones, no lesions or contusions apart from the obvious? What have they been doing to you?" he asked, giving Hrund a frosty look. "You look like you've been being used as a basketball."

"Theo…" Hari said. He knew he should have felt relief. In fact, he felt anything but. His tolerance for surprises was beginning to run thin. "What is all this? You *know* these guys?"

For answer, Chalmers pointed toward a skin tent that had apparently been hastily erected during Hari's escape attempt.

"Take him in there, please," he told the *daitya*. "*Gently*. And then go find something to do. Dr. Chandrasekaran and I would like to have our conversation in private."

***

Olga's village was not located far from the swamp, a cluster of crude huts of moss and woven branches. Men and women in the same Cro-Magnon chic Olga favored strode around on various errands. A few glanced curiously at the newcomers, but most ignored them. In a corner, a group of riding raptors moved behind a stone corral, watching the newcomers with curious eyes. A group of children played with a baby *horgrym*, laughing and stroking it as it honked.

In front of one of the huts, two men sat at a table made of a roughly hewn log with two smaller logs for stools. A checkerboard had been set up on top and the two sat staring down at it with ferocious concentration. One was evidently from Olga's tribe, a big fellow with a bristling red beard. The other was a skinny fellow in cut-offs and a worn Yale T-shirt with a bald head and a splendid black beard. As soon as he saw Pliny, he leapt to his feet and caught her up in a hug, which she returned so powerfully he nearly toppled over backward.

"Careful, careful," he said, laughing. "You're going to break my back here!"

Monica smiled. "She thought you were in the belly of a gorgonopsian. You can't blame her, Lenny."

"Better a gorgonopsian than a shark," Lenny said ruefully, jerking a thumb at the smiling caveman. "That guy's supposed to be the village headman. He's a doggone cheater, is what he is. Worse than this old guy I used to play with back in Central Park. Don't tell him I said that, by the way."

The bearded man was introduced to Dirk as Lenny Stein, a linguist who had been part of the expedition. A moment later, they were joined by two others—a grey-haired woman with sharp blue eyes and a heavy-set, quiet-spoken man, bald except for a fringe of brown hair. The woman was Anya Dvorak, the man Paul Ruddington. They were introduced by their specialties as well as their names, but by then, Dirk was completely lost as to who did what. Too many syllables for him to keep up with. He wasn't the only one, apparently; Lenny's chess partner was soon beating a retreat to the raptor corral.

All of the scientists knew Pliny, and all of them appeared to know Chalmers in some capacity, some better than others. He came up in the initial conversation a few times, sometimes with indulgent laughter, sometimes with head-shaking and rolled eyes. Dirk had the impression Chalmers had made it his business to seek out prominent people in specific fields and get to know them. *He must have been planning the expedition for some time*, Dirk thought.

"Isn't this fabulous?" Pliny beamed as they seated themselves. "Isn't this wonderful? It bears out all of Grandfather's theories."

"Most of them, yes," Anya said. Despite her name, her accent wouldn't have been out of place in a Hamptons resort, though like the others, she was casually dressed in jeans and a T-shirt. She struck Dirk as both down-to-earth and responsible, and probably served as the group's impromptu den mother.

"I have to admit, it's amazing. These people, for example," Anya went on, nodding at Olga, who was approaching them, idly chewing on a centipede leg. "They're the only true example of mammalian life we've found down here so far. Most of the megafauna and higher lifeforms seem to be some species of dinosaur or reptilian, with a few big insects and arthropods mixed in—most of them from wildly differing periods and even locales."

"But what are they, exactly?" Pliny asked. "Cro-Magnons?"

Ruddington shook his head gloomily. The man had been mostly silent throughout their exchange. He wasn't exactly impolite, but Dirk kept imagining a tiny black cloud floating over his head. He wondered if the guy lectured at whatever university he was affiliated with; if he did, Dirk pitied his students.

"That's a question for the labs. We're in no position to do genetic profiles. Without our equipment, we can't even draw blood samples—assuming they'd let us. They *look* like contemporary humans, but for all we know, they could be a completely different species. There were a number of those, you know, not just Cro-Mags and Neanderthals."

"I haven't had a chance to do a deep dive into their language yet," Lenny said. "I can't even tell what they call themselves. The dinosaurs are all something-something-*grym*, I do know *that*. *Horgrym, marlgrym, thamgrym, aitgrym, brothazgrym*..."

"Ha, ha," Anya said drily.

"They're like the *yaksha*," Pliny said excitedly. "That was the name my grandfather had given in his book to a theoretical

Patalan people, a less technologically advanced slave-race used by the *Naga*s."

"And we haven't happened upon any of *them*," Lenny said. "Which is fine by me, let me tell you."

"I'm with you on that," Anya put in, "but the possibility of their existence isn't something we can ignore forever. Theo had actual physical proof of the *mani* stones. It now seems most of his theories were at least mostly on target, and that being so, there may be other races down here that might prove quite a bit less friendly to us. We also don't know what the rays from that big artificial sun might be doing to us, quite apart from how the buggers got it up there in the first place.

"I've been arguing that it's in our best interest to get back up to the surface and return with a properly-accoutered and non-invasive research party."

Lenny snorted. "And *I've* argued that we can't get a team of any kind properly 'accoutered' until we have some real idea what we're dealing with down here."

"That's right," Monica said eagerly. "We can learn far more by lying low and exploring for a month or two."

"That could also get us slaughtered," Ruddington grumbled. "Besides, we don't have anything like the necessary equipment for living in the wild for even a week, let alone a month. I'd rather come back prepared for any eventuality than have the information die with us because we went off scrambling half-cocked into the Cretaceous."

Monica giggled. "Oh, Paul, you just want to get back to your lab and your journals."

The chatter continued back and forth. So far, those in favor of cutting the expedition short were outnumbered. Dirk tended to side with them, but no one seemed terribly interested in his thoughts. As the scientists continued their arguments, he got up and slipped away. He'd noticed Olga had made her way toward a fire where segments of centipede were roasting. He guessed this was the best way the tribe had to preserve it. Olga sank down to squat by the hot ashes, poking at a shell with a pointed stick. She didn't seem to be paying Dirk much attention, but when he sank down next to her, she silently handed him a chunk of the white meat.

He balked at first, then sniffed it and gave it a try. It was fibrous, kind of like crab, but much tougher and much less sweet. A tub of drawn butter and lemon would have improved the flavor, but without cows that hardly seemed likely.

Dirk watched her covertly. He was impressed by her rough beauty, but also by how exotic she seemed. After all, this was someone who had never even seen a television or a computer, who had no idea what the internet was. She had never eaten a pizza or drank a beer or seen a movie.

After a time, another woman joined them—this one noticeably older than Olga, but striking in the same nature-girl kind of way. The two exchanged glances and the newcomer sat herself down cross-legged while Olga got up. Dirk guessed she had come to take Olga's place at the smoking fire. A moment later, Olga went padding off over the turf, but not before giving Dirk a covert glance over her shoulder. Not quite a smile, and not quite invitingly…but their eyes met and neither of them looked away. Dirk was aware the older woman was watching him, and she *was* smiling, no question at all.

Dirk found himself getting up and following the *yaksha* huntress. He had a feeling it wasn't a great idea. After all, he knew almost nothing about these people or their customs, and the possibility of unwittingly giving offense—probably of the kill-first, ask-questions-later variety—seemed a little too high for comfort. But he'd never been particularly good at avoiding temptation.

Olga guided him to a section of the camp that was covered with hummocks of grass. A moment later, she threw herself onto the ground beside one of the hummocks and began squirming. Dirk watched, startled; he wondered if she was having a seizure. But there apparently was an entrance of some kind under the grass, and Olga was wriggling inside, like a snake into a hole. For a moment, all he could see were her butt and legs; a moment later, her tough, blackened soles were framed briefly in the opening. Then she was gone entirely.

Taking a deep breath, Dirk got down on the ground and followed as best he could, feeling his way through the short, grassy tunnel into a small interior space. The "ceiling" was just high enough to allow him to sit upright. It was composed of tightly woven thatch, loose enough to allow a little light inside. There were a few personal items set around the place—a bowl of hardened clay, a couple of stone knives, and what appeared to be a raptor's claw, or maybe the tooth of something considerably bigger. And there was Olga, crouched and waiting for him. This time, her smile made her intentions abundantly clear.

A moment later, he was wrapped in her arms and legs. She smelled of smoke and sweat and leather. She was surprisingly gentle; at any other time, Dirk would have found her touch overwhelmingly sexy. Now he found it relaxing as well. It occurred to him he had not slept properly in hours, maybe even an entire day. His excitement was fading, and though he tried desperately to wake himself back up, he was asleep before he knew it.

# EIGHT

"I apologize for this, Hari. Most sincerely. But you have to understand, my hand has been forced by circumstance."

Hari watched Chalmers stirring the fire. The old man sat cross-legged with his back to him. Much of the smoke billowed out of a hole in the upper part of the tent, but some of it lingered, hurting his eyes. Hari sat nearby, trying to rub some of the soreness out of his shoulder.

"Nothing to say?" Chalmers shook his head. "I can't say I blame you. It's an ugly business, and it started moving a good deal too quickly. Of necessity, I was not quite honest with you—with you, or anyone, Pliny included."

"And just where *is* Pliny?" Hari asked. "The last time I saw her, she and that young fellow were running for their lives."

"She's quite safe." The very brief pause between question and answer told Hari all he needed to know.

"You don't know, do you?" It stung Hari's heart to do it, but he said, "Your own granddaughter."

"I told her how to get from the cavern to Patala. There was an ancient mechanism in the cave that provided her with transport. I believe that by now she would have found Anya and the others, who should already be there. If not, then she would have found a *yaksha* village situated near the mechanism I mentioned. They'd have taken her in. They mind their own business, but in general, they're as benevolent as I described them in the book."

"But how can you *know*?"

"She's safe," Chalmers said tersely. "As safe as anyone can be."

Hari sensed the tension in the old man's voice. Pressing him seemed like a less than productive idea. "So it's all real," he said quietly. "Patala. The *Naga*. Energy crystals. Living dinosaurs."

Chalmers gave a little snort of laughter. He still hadn't turned around. "It would be more comfortable if it weren't, I know.

Much nicer to real about this stuff with a good fire before you and a glass of something. Reality is so much *messier*, isn't it, Hari?"

He rose smoothly to his feet, stretching his shoulders with a low popping sound, but not turning around. He began poking at the fire, stirring the ashes.

"You do know that I found Patala before I wrote the book that so inspired you? Some years ago, that was. Completely by accident. The dinosaurs, the different castes or races…all of them were pre-existing fact from which I later constructed the 'theory' in my book. If anything, I had to play down some of the more lurid stuff. No one would have believed it otherwise. Of course they didn't anyway. If I didn't have money of my own to promote my ideas, they'd have gone down the shitter. Just another crank writing paperbacks about lost civilizations. But even with money, all I am is a crank who's treated with slightly more respect than the average man.

"And as is usually the way with these things, the situation has become more difficult over time, not less. I'm in rather deep just now. So you'll have to forgive me for being a bit less than the man you're used to dealing with."

Finally, he turned. Hari now saw that Chalmers had been stirring the fire not with a stick, but a pair of tongs. Something shining and smoking was gripped in the tongs. A *mani* stone.

Chalmers truly didn't look like the man Hari knew. His long face seemed pained. "I don't want to do this. It was never meant for you. I can't say any more right now. But it needs to be done. The *daitya* demand it, among other reasons."

"Thought you were their great white leader, Theo."

Chalmers shook his head ruefully. "Hardly. Call this a security measure. If you hadn't tried to make a break for it…" He shook his head again.

Chalmers said something in a loud, sharp voice, and two *daitya* entered the tent and seized Hari by the shoulders. He struggled, but it did him no good; even if he were rested and full of energy, the *daitya* had a great deal on him in terms of weight and strength. One man reached for Hari's chest and roughly tore his shirt open, exposing his chest.

Chalmers came forward, holding out the stone. Heat radiated from it in shivering waves. "It won't be pleasant, I'm afraid, and I've nothing to offer you for the pain. I'm told liquor doesn't do much good anyway. All I can say is that they would prefer I give you considerably more than one stone."

Hari yelled. There wasn't much else he could do. Then when the hot, glassy surface of the jewel kissed his flesh, the yells turned to screams. By the time the *daitya* let him fall to the ground, his throat was aching and he could manage nothing but a harsh whispering cry. But the pain continued.

\*\*\*

Paul Ruddington opened the first-aid kit and stared down at the four lumps of glowing crystal nestled inside on a bed of gauze. He had managed to seize the kit up before the pale men appeared in the cave and hustled them into the "elevator." He had played along with his colleagues, affecting the same chattering fascination with their captors. But he cared nothing for them or for the strange reptilian creatures that accompanied them. All he cared about were the crystals.

Only one of the stones was his. Chalmers had given one to each of the scientists once he'd convinced them to go on this crazy expedition. All of them were interested in the crystals, but he was the team's sole geologist; it hadn't been particularly difficult to convince the others to let him store them together in the empty kit.

Ruddington knew the stones were something unusual. He had taken every opportunity to examine them, but could find no explanation for the strange light that surged up in them in time with his own pulse. He had a vague idea—the suspicion of a habitually suspicious man—that they were not of particularly good quality. That Chalmers was having them on, tossing them scraps. They certainly weren't of the same caliber as the *mani* stones described in his book.

Even so, he had to have them. Something in him responded to the stones, *wanted* them. What had Chalmers said about them? They were an energy source, and a means of focusing energy. He needed to have them tested in a proper lab—by trustworthy people, of course. But he was sure they were worth millions, whatever their comparative quality.

And they were more than his payment. Right now, they were his means of escape.

He shut and latched the metal box, then moved carefully out of the hut that he was sharing with Lenny. By now, most of the party was asleep—it was difficult falling asleep in an environment where it always seemed to be high noon, but they were slowly acclimating. They had no reason to suspect the *yaksha* would turn on them, but they made certain that one of their party was always awake in case they got frisky. Ruddington had volunteered take the first watch, and no one had objected.

Lenny was sprawled on a pallet of dried grass on the hut's floor, snoring his lungs out. The old man's granddaughter was chattering away with Monica in the hut set aside for her and Anya. Anya was most likely sleeping as well in her hut. The lunkhead who'd accompanied Pliny was nowhere to be seen—probably trying his luck with one of the *yaksha* women. Paul snorted. Good luck to him. He'd approached one of the wenches himself shortly after their arrival and was lucky not to have gotten his throat slit. Probably even luckier Anya hadn't found out about it, blue-nosed old bitch that she was.

A few of the *yaksha* were moving about the camp. They watched him curiously, but made no attempt to approach or stop him as he walked stealthily away.

He didn't like this place. Cave people and dinosaurs living together might be fascinating from a purely scientific standpoint, but they made him feel like he was trapped in a Saturday morning cartoon. All he had to do was get back to the elevator. He knew the stones powered the thing; he had seen the crystals set into the *daitya*'s flesh flashing when the inner chamber sealed itself and began moving. It might take him some time, but he was certain he could work the same trick with the stones he carried with him. Once he was safely back in the world above, he could see to his colleagues' rescue…once he'd figured out what to do with the crystals, that was. In the meantime, they didn't seem to be in any serious danger.

He walked until the smoke of the campfire was a blue haze in the distance behind him. Then he began looking for the tall spire of stone that housed the elevator. It *should* have been visible on the flat terrain, even from here, but a fog had risen, hiding everything more than a mile or so away.

He couldn't see it. Perhaps he was going the wrong way. He veered north, but that didn't seem to do him any good. By then he was becoming nervous, suspicious that he was now getting more and more lost. Chambers' inner world was no place to lose your way in. The examples of local fauna he'd seen on their initial explorations had been more than enough to convince him of that. Occasionally, a loud, shrieking cry sounded from the surrounding mist. Nothing emerged to threaten him, but he was getting steadily more agitated.

After a certain amount of aimless wandering, Ruddington opened the kit. If Chalmers was right, the *mani* stones controlled just about everything in this strange place. Maybe they could help him find his way.

When he tried lifting one of the stones, he was surprised to see that the four had fused together somehow. They pulsed in his hand so brightly he almost dropped them in panic. The stones buzzed faintly in his fingers, vibrating steadily like one of those signals you were given in restaurants to let you know when your table was ready. It occurred to him that the stones were signaling something…or someone. He dropped the stones back into the box and shut it again, scowling. Minerals weren't alive or intelligent, no matter what all the New Age morons out there believed.

Still, Ruddington wasn't entirely surprised several moments later, when a loud, lowing noise sounded from his right. He could see figures in the distance, slowly approaching him. He was relieved at first, believing them to be *yaksha*, come to take him back to the village. The girls must have woken up and panicked when they found him gone.

He peered at the group of figures, shielding his eyes against the sun-stone's increasing glare. The party was comprised of a couple of the big quadrupedal dinosaurs—*horgryms*, the *yaksha* called them. But these were far bigger than the ones the *yaksha* used as riding animals and beasts of burden; each carried several *daitya*, while others walked along beside them. In the middle of the party was a truly enormous dino, much like the *horgryms* in shape, but two or three times as large. It bore a kind of silk howdah on its back, swaying as it walked.

Paul felt a prickle of unease undermining his initial relief. Most of the *daitya* were armed, carrying spears or machetes. They looked more like a military unit than a search party—and of course, there was no reason to believe the *daitya* had any interest in his well-being.

Finally, the party was close enough to approach him. A big, ugly fellow in a kilt of tanned dino-leather with matching sandals made a chopping gesture at the other *daitya*, who began moving past Ruddington. It occurred to him they were making their way to the *yaksha* village, and they probably weren't going to exchange recipes. The largest dino with the howdah remained where it was, the big *daitya* standing beside it.

It was just the two of them now. The *daitya* smiled down at him—not in a particularly threatening way, but not in a particularly pleasant way, either. Paul cleared his throat.

"Can you help me?" he asked. "I want to go home. Home," he added, pointing a finger skyward.

The *daitya*'s smile widened and he extended a hand, the fingers curling a little. The fellow's eyes were fixed on the first-aid kit, and it didn't take a linguist to understand him. *Why don't you give me that pretty box, little man? Give it to me and maybe everything will be alright. Maybe* you'll *be alright.*

Paul handed him the box, boiling with rage inside but without any hesitation or signs of defiance. He had been in this situation before, after all. If he could get back all the lunch money and candy money and comic book money he had willingly handed over to bullies over the years, he could probably afford a new car.

"Very good," the man said, in thickly accented but perfectly understandable English. "Part of the keystone. Very important. These were lost to us for a very long time. Very good of you, sair." Paul was taken aback, but rallied quickly.

"You can understand me? Will you take me home? Please? I don't care about the jewels. I just want to go home."

For answer, the *daitya* turned his placid smile on the howdah. A hand slid from between the silken coverings and made a lazy, beckoning gesture.

"The Lord wishes to see you," the *daitya* said, grinning broadly.

"Lord?" Paul didn't like the look of either the *daitya*'s smile or the "Lord's" hand. The latter was a whitish-green, its fingers alternately long and stubby, with pointed ends. It was either encased in a glove or its skin was inhumanly thick and leathery. The sight of it made Paul feel faintly sick.

"But why...?" Paul let his voice trail off. He didn't think he was going to get out of this. He stepped up to the howdah and the *daitya*, looking pleased, pulled the silks back, fully revealing the being inside.

"Oh my God..." Paul was overwhelmed by a wave of sweetish odor he took to be some version of perfume, underlaid by a musky smell that seemed familiar and also deeply unpleasant. The zoo...the last time he'd smelled something like that had been at the reptile house at the zoo.

But seeing but was far worse than the smell. Paul, unwisely, tried to make a break for it, but the *daitya* caught his arm without difficulty, holding him fast.

If Paul had some means of cutting his arm off, he would gladly have done it. He didn't want to look at the thing in the howdah. He didn't want to be anywhere near it.

But he was being dragged back toward the silken chamber. The thing there was reaching for him. A moment later, the pain started. It was quite a while before it—and everything else— ended.

***

Lenny woke when the pale-skinned men barged into his hut. They seemed to be searching for something—or someone—but they didn't seem interested in him, and after a few cursory kicks at the sections of log that served as furniture, they simply grunted and left.

Going back to sleep wasn't an option. He could hear loud cries outside—he recognized Anya's voice raised in an indignant shout and shrill cries of panic that could only have been made by Monica. He got up and hurriedly pulled on his shorts and running shoes. Not exactly a warrior's armor, but it would have to do.

He realized suddenly that Paul was gone. Had the *daitya* taken him? *Not likely, if they left me. Let's face it, I'm better-looking.* Before leaving the hut, Lenny cast a quick glance at the pile of dried grass where Paul had hidden the first-aid kit containing the *mani* stones Chalmers had given them. No sign of it. *Interesting.* But no time to play detective now.

Lenny slipped out of the slit in the hut's grass-covered side that served as a door. Outside were a number of *daitya*, three of whom were dragging Pliny, Monica, and Anya along by their shoulders toward an enormous waiting *horgrym*. None of the women were going quietly. Pliny was trying her earnest best to stomp on her *daitya*'s foot, while Anya was struggling and shouting threats that Lenny thought could probably be heard all the way back in the upper world. Monica was wailing and crying; poor kid, she'd always struck Lenny as a gentle soul, not used to any kind of harsh treatment.

The villagers stood nearby, watching solemnly as their guests were removed. It was clear to Lenny that no help was going to come from them. Instead of wasting his time, he ran up to the *daitya*, focusing on the poor fellow who was dragging the screeching Pliny along—he had his hands full more than his companions and might be a little more willing to listen to reason.

"Hey! Hey, there! 'Scuse me, comrade! A word?" Lenny wished earnestly that he could have learned at least a few words of the *daitya*'s language. It would surely have made his job easier. But the *daitya* just stomped along with his eyes averted.

"Hey!" Out of options, Lenny jumped in front of the man, his arms extended to either side with palms showing. *I come in peace, see? No weapons*. Not that this poor Brooklyn boy would know anything about throwing a punch, let alone wielding a *daitya* short-sword. The big man stopped abruptly, staring down at Lenny with glowering contempt.

Lenny smiled sunnily, foolish enough to believe this represented some kind of progress. "Hey *bubi*, how's by you? How about we talk about this, huh? You don't want these girls, take it from me. More trouble than they're worth, especially this little one. Maybe we go grab an egg cream, work something out, whaddaya say?"

"Lenny, *no!*" Pliny screamed. She kicked against the *daitya*, digging her nails into his arm, but it was too late. The *daitya* had already unsheathed his blade and thrust it into Lenny's gut.

Lenny stared down at the beefy hand holding the hilt of the sword that was now inside him. With a sudden shock of pain, the blade was pulled out. Blood trickled, then gushed—first from the wound, then from his mouth. As the *daitya* dragged their prey off, he fell to his knees, gagging.

*So this is how it ends*. Lenny remained in a kneeling position until he fell onto his side. Just before it all went dark, he remembered his father, a grey-haired, perpetually unhappy man. After Lenny's *bar mitzvah*, he'd hugged his son close, kissed his cheek, and whispered a word of advice. *They always get you in the end. You can't avoid it.*

***

Dirk woke out of a dream in which everyone he'd ever known in his life was fighting, a savage knock-down fist-fight, with everyone shouting and determined to lay all the others in their graves.

He woke up suddenly, with a hoarse gasp, and when he saw himself surrounded by thatch and bunched moss of Olga's hidey-hole, he nearly panicked, unsure of where he was. *Oh, that's right. I'm trapped in a subterranean prehistoric world with a bunch of crazy women.*

Of Olga herself, there was no sign. He had no idea how long he'd slept—his phone said 3:00, but that might equally well have been PM or AM. But he felt a great deal better. He could have eaten one of the *horgryms*, spit-roasted with a side of beans and cornbread.

It was also evident to him that nothing had happened between himself and Olga during his stay in the cave; there was no sign that his shirt had even been removed, let alone his shorts.

There didn't seem to be much point in hanging around, so he set about squirming his way out of the entrance, not doing the cave as a whole much good in the process. Outside, there was no real sign of any kind of altercation, though there were far more *yaksha* around than he had seen earlier. They gave him strange suspicious glances—more sour than confrontational. If they disapproved of him sleeping with Olga, they gave no sign of it.

Olga herself came ambling up to him, with the same half-angry expression on her face, a large, freshly caught fish gripped in one hand and a spear in the other. Before he could greet her, she said, in oddly accented English, "Your friends gone."

Dirk blinked. "What? I thought you...how do you speak English suddenly?" She couldn't have learned the language in the short time Monica & Co. were here. While he was still processing that, something else occurred to him. "What do you mean they're *gone?*"

"*Daitya* take."

Dirk stared at her. "The guys with the funny complexions? They just…took them?"

"*Daitya* do what *daitya* do." She shrugged. "Take them to *Naga* City, I think."

"And they went willingly?" It wasn't entirely impossible, given the scientists'—to his mind—perverse need to explore every aspect of this strange world, including "*Naga* City"…and what the hell *was* "*Naga* City," anyway?

"No," Olga said emphatically. "Did not want to go. Went screaming. Cry like babies. But *daitya* strong." She sank down to a cross-legged pose and began gutting the fish. She slid a hand into the fish's open belly and hauled out a palmful of glistening roe, which she offered to Dirk.

"Taste good," she said, patting her belly with her free hand.

"Olga, we've got to get them back!" His mind was a whirl of guilt and self-recrimination.

"Why?" Olga gave him a suspicious glare as she tucked into the fish eggs. "You like little woman?" He wasn't sure if she was referring to Pliny in particular, or if "little woman" was her general name for any female not of the *yaksha*. "Little woman your *googa?*"

"No. No, she's not my *googa* or whatever. But she's my…friend? I'm responsible for her. Do you understand?"

He wasn't really Pliny's bodyguard, and he certainly didn't feel responsible for Chalmers' team of scientists. But if they had been snatched away, he shouldn't have been sleeping. He should have been taken with them—or at least badly injured in trying to prevent the *daitya*'s raid.

But it was clear from Olga's munching, egg-smeared face that she very much did not understand.

"Oh, God. Never mind. Which way did they go?"

Olga kept munching, her eyes focused on his, but not revealing much. Finally, not seeing any better alternative, Dirk got up and began walking away from the Olga and the *yaksha* village. He had no idea if he was going in the right direction, but it seemed the most likely option. A minute or two later, something swatted his shoulder, hard enough to make him stumble. Olga, wiping the last of the egg from her mouth with the back of her hand, was beside him, spear in hand.

"We go," she said. "Together."

Dirk wanted to just shrug, but he knew he wasn't going to be able to pull it off properly. Besides, the prospect of having Olga at his side was comforting, however much he might deny it. At least she knew where *Naga* City was. "Alright," he said, and off they went. Olga walked slightly behind him, but when he started veering off the straight track, she hit the back of his legs with her spear.

# NINE

The next morning, Chalmers checked Hari's chest. Hari didn't resist. The pain had subsided to a dull ache that had kept him from sleeping, as it had ruled out any further chances of trying to escape. When he lifted his head and looked down at the *mani* stone, he saw it had sunken into the flesh of his chest, as though it had been pressed into soft clay—not deeply, but firmly enough to make the prospects of its removal unlikely. A dim light was pulsing in it, seeming to keep time with his breathing and heartbeat.

"Good. It's going well," Chalmers said, standing up. "You should eat something. This next phase of the trip won't be easy. Or pleasant—at least not for me. Maybe you have a stronger stomach."

"Why? Where're we going?"

"The *Naga*s' city. There's an entrance some distance from here, in a volcano. We're taking the *Garuda*."

"I see what you mean about it not being a pleasant trip."

Chalmers didn't offer any answer to that. He was striding around the camp, talking to Hrund and overseeing the packing up of the tents.

"Just tell me one thing, yeah? How does this rock work?"

"What do you mean?"

"I've read your book, Theo. Ten times, last count. And Pliny told me what it did to the *daitya* at the hotel. It's a mind-control device? Am I your slave now?"

"No, you're certainly not. Using the stones to actually control someone is certainly possible, but it requires that a number of them be implanted at once. We won't take that step with you. It's not necessary for my purposes, and the *daitya* won't insist if you don't give them reason. Frankly, I'd rather you didn't."

"So what's the point of it, then? So far as the *daitya* are concerned, I mean. I know better now than to ask you about your 'purposes.'"

He meant the remark to sting, but Chalmers' face remained impassive. "I said it's not for mind control, and it isn't. But it can cause pain if you try to run. I wouldn't advise it."

A *daitya* brought a duplicate of the previous night's meal on a leather plate. Hari got up wincing. "You're a prince, Theo."

The *Garuda* sat by in the background, seeming to watch him.

*Air Pteranodon*, Hari thought sourly, picking at the slab of bread. *Won't this be fun?*

It wasn't, as it happened. Not at all.

\*\*\*

They must have walked for hours. Dirk was increasingly aware of not having had a bath or change of clothes for more than two days. He had never worried too much about such things, but it had gotten really bad; it felt as though he'd rolled in mud and it had baked onto his skin. Tiny flies followed them in twin clouds, buzzing annoyingly in Dirk's ears and causing him endless aggravation as they landed and crept on his skin.

Olga didn't seem to notice, possibly because her own condition left Dirk's well behind—it struck him that she may never have had a bath, not once in her life. She strode along calmly, tossing her spear from hand to hand and humming tunelessly to herself.

They were crossing a vast flat plain, lit by the sky-stone. Far to the east were mountains, the highest peaks of which actually connected to Patala's rocky ceiling. *Naga* City? Possibly, though Olga only shrugged when he asked her directly. Sometimes Dirk convinced himself that he could see tiny figures ahead of them, which he thought were probably the *daitya* raiding party, carrying their prizes back home. Other times, he couldn't see them at all and told himself that the whole effort was self-delusion on his part.

Specimens of the local wildlife popped up occasionally to say hello. Small bipedal dinosaurs would rush them from stands of tall grass, hissing and venting steam-whistle shrieks. Olga ran them off effortlessly, slashing out with her spear and kicking at them. Some tried to stand their ground, but when Olga neatly decapitated one such, the ambushes trailed off noticeably.

Olga sat down cross-legged in the grass and began slaughtering the animal. "Shouldn't we keep going?" Dirk fretted.

"Hungry," Olga explained, patting her belly. If nothing else, *yaksha* women were apparently blessed with limitless appetites. She cut the little dino's flesh into pale strips which she ate raw, like sashimi. Dirk tried a couple at her urging. They actually tasted pretty good, though every TV documentary on internal parasites he'd ever seen started running themselves through his mind.

"So what are the *Naga*s, anyway?" Dirk asked finally, stifling a sour belch.

Olga scowled. "*Naga*s bad," she said, shaking her head.

"Yeah, I gathered that much. But *why*? What *are* they?" For answer, Olga lifted both hands, set them palm on palm, and swiveled them through the air, making a snakelike hissing sound.

"O-okay…" But he had apparently caught Olga in a talkative mood. She sat back on her heels, wiping her blood-smeared hands on the grass.

"Long time ago, *Naga*s *make* Patala. All this," she said, making a circular gesture that encompassed everything from the sun-stone to the far-off mountains. "Things bad in the other world, *Naga*s needed place to hide. They bring animals here, the *gryms* first, later the *daitya* and *yaksha*."

Dirk didn't particularly feel like tackling the question of why Olga seemed content to lump her own people in with "animals." "Why'd they do that?"

Olga smiled and rubbed her belly meaningfully.

"Oh. So…they, the *Naga*…weren't people like you. The *yaksha*."

Olga did the snake-head move again, hissing loudly.

"Yeah, okay. I gotcha. So…that's why they wanted my friends?" The idea of Pliny being eaten made him feel sick, though an inappropriately hilarious image suddenly came into his mind of Pliny on a platter, chattering indignantly as she was basted with sauce. He was afraid if he allowed himself to start laughing, he wouldn't be able to stop.

Olga shook her head, turning her palms out in a gesture that clearly said, *I don't know.*

"*Naga*s strange. Sometimes they take *yaksha*. The old people say it never for food. But nobody know why."

"And why do you take it? I mean, can't you fight back?"

"*Yaksha* try fight," Olga said glumly. "Many times. Always lose."

"So why are you coming along with me now?"

Olga gave him a wide, gap-toothed grin and poked his ribs. "Don't know. Maybe Olga like you." With that, she got up and started walking again, leaving the carcass behind her.

Sighing, Dirk followed her, unsure of whether he was flattered or freshly terrified.

***

Pliny had been entertaining herself by making faces at the *daitya* who had been set to guard them. She had been warned several times by a nervous Monica not to provoke the man, but his puzzled expression at her crossed eyes and rolled tongue was so comical that she couldn't resist. Even Anya got a chuckle out of them. Still, their situation as a whole wasn't that amusing.

Poor Lenny was dead. Despite his efforts, they had killed him without a second thought. The three women had been taken without a fight and put in a howdah on top of a *horgrym* that was probably twice the size of the others they had seen. The howdah amounted to a small room with silken walls that shifted constantly as the beast walked. The *daitya* who was watching them didn't seem interested in hurting them, but even Pliny didn't give them much of a chance were they to try and run.

"Where do you think they're taking us?" Pliny asked, for perhaps the fifth time.

"I'm guessing to their place of residence," Anya said. "After that, who knows? All we can do is keep an eye out for possible means of escape. If one comes up, then at least one of us needs to try and leave and get back to the *yaksha* village. That's the safest place we know of. Try to find a way to contact Chalmers. Our phones aren't much good down here, but we'll think of something."

Eventually, the journey came to an end…or at least the *grym* stopped its shambling gait. This came at roughly the same time the outside light suddenly went dark, as though a blanket had suddenly been thrown over the sun.

"What's this, now?" Anya asked. She seemed more nervous than previously, especially when a *daitya* outside pulled open the screen. Outside, it was completely dark, except for occasional illumination from torches carried past. Their guard stood up and gestured brusquely at the gap in the silks.

"Outside," he said. Pliny was startled to hear him speaking English, but he didn't look to be in any mood to discuss the subject. So she just took the opportunity to give him another face before leading the others out. They were in a huge cavern, surrounded with the plus-sized *horgryms* and torch-bearing *daitya*. Some distance behind them, Pliny could see an opening onto the outside, the sun-stone's dim light still filtering through. A set of wooden stairs had been pushed up to their *horgrym*, which now lay with both sets of legs stretched out like a reclining elephant.

Pliny took her time descending, all the while keeping her mind focused on the cave entrance. She remembered what Anya said about making an escape when an opportunity presented itself; it didn't seem likely a better one would come along. She allowed herself to tense a little with each step, and then she reached the cavern floor, she let the tension explode out of her in the form of a savage kick to the groin of the nearest *daitya*. He fell over with a loud *whoomph*, clutching at his guts as Pliny made for the entrance.

Several *daitya* tried to grab her, but she swerved past them without much trouble. They apparently hadn't even considered she might try an escape attempt.

Something large and bulky crept out of the shadows, slithering into her path. At first, Pliny thought it was another species of *grym*, but when the light hit it, she nearly fell over in her eagerness not to come in contact with it.

It was unlike anything she had ever seen before.

It was like a huge, grossly obese human figure draped with rotting sheets of tapestry, all worked with pearls and small jewels. But it didn't have legs. From the waist down, its body became a slug-like monstrosity, but scaled rather than slimy. The thing's face was veiled with more of the tapestry, but it lifted a heavy, scaled hand to pull them aside and confront Pliny face to face. She wished it hadn't.

The thing's features were human enough, but its mouth was lipless, revealing long, sharpened teeth that were more like daggers. Its eyes were slit-pupiled and utterly devoid of expression. Small glittering *mani* stones had been implanted here and there in its pasty, scaly skin.

It spoke to her, a hissing, gargling noise that must have been a language, but sounded like nothing Pliny had ever heard. That was enough. She let the *daitya* guard grab her by the arm and pull her away.

The slug-serpent thing watched her narrowly. Pliny had an idea that the thing was as disgusted by her as she was by it. Anya and Monica held her.

"Come," the *daitya* said—not really smugly, but with a certain ugly conviction. He seemed sure she wouldn't chance making another break for it. He was right.

"It's awful. Oh God, Pliny, what is that?" Monica gasped, as the three were led away.

"It must be a *Naga*," Pliny whispered. She remembered sitting at the family vacation home in the Hamptons, listening to her grandfather tell her stories about the Serpent Kings. She had sat wide-eyed, devouring every word. Afterward, she had torn around the yard, armed with a stick, playing that she was Hanuman or Rama.

"It certainly was," Anya said. She sounded horrified and at the same time fascinated. She couldn't stop looking over her shoulder at the thing. "But Monica's question stands: what the hell *is* it? Something like that never evolved naturally out of saurian stock. It puts old Russell's dinosauroid theory to shame. Did you see the hindquarters?"

"Like a huge slug," Monica said hoarsely, shuddering a little in mingled disgust and fascination.

"I'd guess something more akin to an actual snake, but quite a bit heavier—the musculature must be massive. But it would have to be, to support the thing's weight. And the face..."

The *daitya* behind them gave Anya a shove. The older woman shut up promptly, though she turned a savage glance over one shoulder at the man. "We should table this discussion for later," she muttered.

Pliny barely heard her. Her body was plodding through the increasingly dark tunnels of the *Naga*s' world, but inside, she was back in Nags' Head. Sometimes the *Naga*s in Grandfather's stories were wicked beyond anything humans could imagine; at other times, they helped the heroes and showed the human race great kindness. There wasn't much question which side the thing she had just seen was on.

***

Air Pteranodon was truly not much fun.

The *Garuda* had been kitted out with an enormous harness of leather. Three heavy braided straps hung from either side, each one worked into a kind of tubular leather cage, large enough to hold a passenger: Chalmers, Hari, Hrund, and three other *daitya*. An older, weathered *daitya* who was missing an eye sat between the creature's shoulders, guiding it through some interaction of his *mani* stones with those set in the creature's flesh.

Hari had no idea how far up they were. He didn't want to know. He kept his eyes squeezed tightly shut the entire trip— Chalmers had advised this, but Hari didn't need to be pressed. He had never been particularly fond of flying, but up to now, he wasn't actually phobic. He had a feeling that would change— assuming he survived.

The duration of the trip was something else he was unclear on. After the initial nightmare of jostling and swinging settled down, the trip settled into a long ordeal of being buffeted by cold winds, the flapping of the *Garuda*'s wings echoing in his mind. Once only, when he thought he felt the *Pteranodon* beginning to descend, he opened his eyes. He shut them immediately. Jagged mountain peaks were directly beneath him; they looked close enough for him to kick stones off.

To keep his mind off the trip, he tried to focus on the pain of the stone in his chest, but that seemed to make it grow worse. Remembering his childhood in London was better—his grandmother's curry, reading in his room, telly at night. But in time, he grew depressed. Multiplication tables were better, and then he tried reconstructing in his mind certain articles he'd read.

At some point, the feeling of descending returned. They were dropping, quickly and steadily. For the second and last time until they landed, Hari chanced opening his eyes.

What he saw was another mountain, but this one looked as though some bored deity had taken an enormous knife and sliced off the top, leaving a vast black cavity. They were going down into this, deeper and deeper, but no matter how deep they went, Hari saw nothing.

# TEN

As they walked, Dirk discovered that keeping track of time in Patala was weirdly difficult. He hadn't realized how much he had depended upon the movements of the sun to orient himself. Here it was always high noon, and he found himself constantly checking his watch. His phone said they had been traveling nearly a day, but he couldn't escape the feeling that it might have been a much longer—or shorter—period of time.

Olga, predictably enough, didn't seem worried. She soldiered on as though they were enjoying a summer hike. Only once did she break out of her tuneless humming. Something rustled in the nearby grass, and she stopped immediately, her entire body gone tense. She poked at the tussock of grass with her spear— tentatively at first, then more forcefully.

Something leapt out at them—it looked a bit like the small bipeds they had dealt with earlier, but much slimmer in build, with grotesquely large, goggling eyes that seemed to take up most of its skull. More disturbingly, a single fist-sized *mani* stone was implanted in its chest. The thing stood its ground, hissing at them like a tea kettle.

Dirk stepped back, lifting his crowbar warningly. Olga didn't hesitate. She thrust her spear at the thing, missing only by a hair. It bounded off across the grass with a shriek and Olga was right on its heels. The thing might have gotten away if it hadn't repeatedly broken its stride with awkward leaps into the air, its small arms thrashing. *It's trying to fly*, Dirk thought dully. Whether it ever would have made it quickly became a moot point—Olga's spear cut it down in mid-leap.

Dirk stepped up to her, crowbar in hand. "Are you that hungry?" he asked dubiously.

Olga prodded at the creature's limp body with one bare foot. The *mani* stone in the thing's chest glittered once and went dark. "Eyes," Olga said darkly.

"Eyes...you mean this thing is a spy?" It sounded ridiculous, but after all, he had no idea what the stones could and couldn't do. If they could be used to control the men who'd come after them, why couldn't they serve as some kind of camera...or maybe a primitive recording device?

"A spy for who, though?"

"*Naga* use," Olga said darkly. With that, she turned and started walking again, leaving the small corpse behind.

***

At some point, the steady descent stopped. Hari's body came up against a stone floor—hard enough to knock the wind out of him, but not so hard as to make him fear permanent damage had been done.

They were in a huge cavern, lit dimly by *mani* stones on the walls. *Daitya* roamed around on various errands. Gorgonopsians stalked around, growling and glaring suspiciously at them. The *daitya* who'd piloted the *Garuda* released Hari and Chalmers from their bonds with a few quick cuts of his stone knife.

"Well," Chalmers said, stretching. "I've had worse flights. Not many, though. How are you holding up, Hari?"

"I'll live, I suppose," Hari said shortly. "What is this place? Sort of a helipad for pterosaurs?"

"You could call it that. We're still a good ways above Patala proper. The *daitya* use this cavern as a waystation for their peregrinations in and out. You'll be glad to know we'll be walking the rest of the way."

"Yeah, cheers." Hari was busy looking around the place. There wasn't much to see. The cave's walls were lined irregularly with round doorways, each of which was large enough to allow the *Garuda* to fly through them.

"Don't you lot ever worry about your taxi service being seen by the tabloids? 'Giant flying monster seen over badlands'? That kind of thing?"

"Not many people hereabouts. The *Garuda* do get spotted occasionally, but that's our bad luck. So far, it hasn't resulted in any real trouble. People have other things to worry about than a quick glimpse of a flying monster."

Hari was taking that in when several figures emerged from one of the doorways. They weren't *daitya*, though they were nearly as bulky; Hari wasn't sure what they were at first. They moved with a slow, almost undulating motion that confused his eye. They didn't seem to be walking at all. And they were accompanied by bipedal dinosaurs much taller than they—Hari would have put them down as allosaurs. The big animals stalked along without a word, eyeing Chalmers' little party with a silent intensity that was more than a little unnerving.

"Our hosts," Chalmers said tightly. "On your best behavior now, Hari. The *Naga* aren't known for their sense of humor."

"Those are *Naga*?" Hari asked. In spite of himself, he got a little chill, remembering his grandmother's stories. *You told me I'd see them one day, Gran. I guess you were right.*

The *Naga* seemed to be some strange fusion of human and snake, their torsos growing centaur-like from serpentine tails that carried them over the cave floor with sinuous motions. They were considerably paler than even the *daitya*, and most of them seemed to have suffered some kind of facial injury; Hari saw missing eyes, noses, and lips. They were surrounded by a subtle but noticeable perfume, and Hari wondered if it were to mask another, less pleasant odor. They wore elaborate costumes of silk worked with gems and seed pearls.

The *Naga* in the procession's forefront greeted Chalmers with an odd gesture and a stream of fluid syllables. Chalmers responded in kind, though Hari noticed his pronunciation was slightly off. The human mouth possibly wasn't made for the *Naga*s' language.

The lead *Naga* turned his gaze on Hari with an unpleasant, questioning look, as though Chalmers had brought in a mongrel puppy that had just started piddling on the floor. Chalmers said something in *Naga*, and pulled Hari's half-open shirt, revealing the *mani* stone. That seemed to satisfy the *Naga*, though he still didn't look happy. Without another word, the entire procession turned and began moving back toward the cave mouth. Chalmers gestured for Hari to follow with him.

"Sorry about the rough treatment," he said under his breath. "They don't trust humans—they don't exactly adore me, as you can see. I had to reassure them you weren't in a position to cause any difficulties."

"Sure," Hari said tightly. "Hope you put their minds at rest. Hate to cause any trouble." He wasn't sure of his status—was he Chalmers' prisoner, or the *Nagas*'?

The tunnel sloped steadily downward, and they walked for some time—Hari made it an hour, though it was impossible to say with any certainty. Occasionally, they made turns into other tunnels. The way was lit by stones which studded the tunnel walls at regular intervals. Daitya occasionally shouldered past them, sometimes accompanied by gorgonopsians. "Where we going, anyway?"

"Something on the order of a cathedral, mixed with a viewing chamber," Chalmers told him. "It'll give you some idea of the real pecking order around here."

They continued their descent until the tunnel opened up before them onto a vast cylindrical pit, with a ridge running round its circumference. It was like the "helipad," but considerably larger. Like the tunnels, it was illuminated by the flickering light of numerous *mani* stones, but these were not single gems; instead, they were veins of crystal that ran through the stone. Hari glanced upward, but could not see any sign of the sky.

"Try looking down," Chalmers suggested. "That's where the real fun is."

"I'd rather not," Hari said. He didn't like getting too close to the edge of the ridge—it was too easy to imagine a *daitya* running up behind him and giving him a push. But he knew he was better off seeing what was before him. Peering over, he saw the shaft ended far below in a circular floor covered in scattered objects that even at this height he could see were huge saurian bones. He could also see openings of caves set in the wall around the floor that seemed to match in their positions the ones around the pit.

Hari was on the point of asking Chalmers about the bones when the walls of the pit shook. Something very large and very much alive had just cried out. It wasn't the full-throated roar of a dinosaur as heard in movies and cartoons—this was barely audible; he *felt* the cry in every bone of his body, and it was all he could do to keep from turning and running back down the connecting tunnel. Something about the cry put him in a near panic.

"Steady," Chalmers said, taking his arm. The old man looked a little close to panic himself, but he was maintaining self-control, and after a shudder, Hari followed suit. "It's infrasound," Chalmers said. "Very similar effect to what you get with tigers and the like."

Hari was familiar with the idea that large predators' roars worked along a spectrum of sound that could cause prey to freeze or experience paralyzing fear. At the moment, he was more concerned with not wetting himself.

Then he found something else to concern him. The roar's owner was stumbling out of one of the tunnel mouths, into the *mani* light. Hari Chandrasekaran—who had flown on a *Pteranodon* and faced full-grown gorgonopsians—felt close to fainting at the sight of it.

"That's never a tiger," he whispered.

But when he turned to Chalmers, the old man was gone.

***

"Pliny," Pliny said, pointing at herself. "Plin-nee."

"Plifafdafaah," the *Nagina* said, with the patience of a nanny humoring a child. The female *Naga* was at least easier on the eyes than her male counterparts; she was slimmer and her face didn't have any visible scars or deformities. Her silks and decorations were also quite a bit less impressive, and it was the general consensus of the three upworlders that she had been given the task of serving them while at the same time ensuring they did nothing to escape. Pliny had at once seized the opportunity to educate her.

"No," she said patiently. She took the *Nagina*'s unresisting hand and pressed it against her chest. "Plin-nee," she said, then placed her own hand on the *Nagina*'s shoulder. "And you are...?"

"I don't think she's getting it, Plin," Monica said. The three women were seated in a chamber deep within the *Nagas*' city. The room was small but comfortable, the floors strewn with cushions and the walls covered with bright tapestries. Light was provided by the omnipresent *mani* stones, these set into small, lantern-like devices set about the room like candles. There were plates of fruit, which they had set on hungrily—as well as rather less appetizing strips of dried flesh. There were also a number of silken clothes and jewels on offer, which provoked acid comments from Anya on the *Nagas*' opinions of female vanity. Nonetheless, Pliny and Monica had delightedly tried these on, and were now almost as gaudily dressed as their maid.

"I think she understands perfectly," Anya said. "But her oral structure isn't made for English—or probably anything else we might hear spoken in our world, though there might be some basic structural similarities with Urdu. I know some linguists back home who'd give their eyeteeth to spend an hour's conversation with our snaky friend here."

The *Nagina* lowered her eyelashes as though acknowledging her prisoner's interest.

"I just want to know her name," Pliny said irritably. "I should be able to manage that much."

The *Nagina* hesitated, then pressed her hand slightly harder against Pliny, while making an odd, sibilant sound.

Pliny perked up immediately. "What? What was that?"

"It sounded like 'Khresshtra,'" Monica said. "Is that her name?"

"Near enough, anyway," Anya put in. "She must understand us...can't speak the lingo, but she can parse it right enough, hey, Khresshtra?"

"Is that really your name?" Pliny demanded. The *Nagina* hesitated again, then inclined her head in what was clearly the *Naga* version of a nod. This provoked loud squeals of delight from Pliny.

"What's this?" a voice boomed from the doorway. "Language lessons? Hope you've been working on your reptilian, Pliny."

Pliny shrieked with delight at the sight of her grandfather, who stood in the doorway flanked by two sour-faced *Naga* guards. She ran to the old man and buried her face in his chest. "Oh God, Grandfather, where *were* you?"

"I might ask the same question," Anya said coolly. "Really, Theo, I know you like making an entrance, but..."

"Are they going to let us go, Dr. Chalmers?" Monica asked anxiously.

"Of course, my dear," Chalmers said. "In good time, we'll be escorted back to the surface."

"And whose time is 'good time,' exactly?" Anya demanded.

"Grandfather, I lost Dirk," Pliny said miserably. "He wasn't with us when the *daitya* raided the *yaksha* village. Anything could have happened to him."

"Nonsense, Pliny. Mr. Bannerman is a very resourceful young man. Didn't I say so the night we met him? Trust me, I'm an excellent judge of these things."

"Is that a fact?" Anya said coolly. "Let's start with our own situation. Permit me to be a little more direct, Theo: when the hell are your scaly friends going to let us out of here?"

The woman had positioned herself in front of Chalmers, and the two locked eyes. "Never one for subtlety, were you, Anya?" Chalmers chuckled. "Alright, I'll be frank with you. I'm not much more than a prisoner myself right now. The *Naga* hold all the cards. They're the ones with the trained dinosaurs, after all. Their trust of me has always been conditional. I can get you out of here, but until then you have to extend me that same trust."

At that moment, a *Nagina* slithered up to the mouth of the cave entrance. She looked older than Khresshtra, though like her she seemed in much better condition than the males. She was apparently some kind of matron. She gestured at Khresshtra, who took Monica and Pliny by the arms and, half-coaxing, half-pulling, guided them from the chamber.

"Grandfather?" Pliny asked fearfully, looking over her shoulder.

Chalmers made no move to come to her aid, but Pliny saw him clenching and unclenching a fist, his jaw set tightly. "You'll be alright, Pliny. Just do what they say. I've been promised you won't be hurt."

Anya glared at him. "Theo, what the hell is this? She's your granddaughter! Where are they taking her?"

"It'll be alright," Chalmers said, clenching and unclenching his hands as the two girls were removed. "It'll be alright."

# ELEVEN

They approached the mountains of the *Naga* city not long after the incident with the "eye" dino. Dirk didn't like the look of them at all. They erupted from the floor of the plain, their craggy peaks reaching high into the sky. Some of them actually connected to the stony roof of Patala. The sheer faces of the cliffs were riddled with cave entrances, making Dirk think of a gigantic termite colony. What appeared to be a central entrance yawned open in the very front of the peaks.

Olga seemed unimpressed by the mountain, though once they got within a certain distance, she was careful to lead them off to the side, away from the main entrance. Once they had reached the western side of the mountain, she lifted both hands to her mouth and gave a piercing shriek that made Dirk start violently.

"Geez, call out the welcome wagon, why don'cha?" The sound was like the piercing cry of one of the smaller dinosaurs. Olga ignored him, watching the mountains. Eventually, a pale figure emerged from one of the cave mouths, creeping down cautiously. As it drew closer, he could see it was a *yaksha* woman, about the same age and build as Olga. Her tanned skin was blotched with pale patches, and he saw a row of *mani* stones glittering along her side. Her hair was also a bleached, almost-white color, but he had no idea if this was from the *mani* stones or not.

This apparently was a *yaksha* who had been exposed to the same treatment that turned the *daitya* pale. A slave? Olga went up to the woman, making signs Dirk supposed were meant as a greeting. The woman was cautious, but after a time—and some suspicious glares directed at Dirk—she nodded and motioned toward the cave, then started toward it.

Olga went after her and Dirk had no choice but to follow. Inside the cave were a large number of other *yaksha*, both male and female, most much further along in the process of submitting to the *mani* stones' influence. They sat in groups, working at various tasks—pounding or scraping skins, cleaning roots, or carefully twining masses of fiber into rope. One was slaughtering a large animal that looked like a grotesque cross between a crocodile and a bullfrog.

"What's going on here?" Dirk asked. He didn't necessarily expect an answer, but Olga said, "Slaves to *Naga*."

Dirk nodded. This must be what happened to *yaksha* who were abducted by *daitya* raiding parties. "They can't leave because of the stones?"

"More. Slaves are no longer true *yaksha*. No place for them in villages." Olga spoke with a lifted chin and a faintly condescending air. She picked her way among the laboring *yaksha* with a definite attitude; there was no question she considered them inferior to her.

Dirk felt a little shocked by this, but didn't think there was much point in arguing it with Olga. Instead, he said, "Can we like, trust them? If they're the *Naga*s' slaves, won't they call out the guards or something?"

"Slaves are slaves." Olga said loftily. "They work. Nothing else."

"O-okay," Dirk said, continuing to follow her. The cave opened up onto a tunnel in the rear. More *yaksha* came in and out of this, some carrying baskets. Some gave Olga and Dirk distrustful glances; most didn't.

Olga continued padding ahead of him, taking sudden turns here and there until Dirk was completely lost. "Where are we going?" he asked finally.

"Find your *googa*," Olga said, giving him an unpleasant grin. It was the right answer, so far as Dirk was concerned, so he didn't bother correcting her about the nature of his relationship with Pliny. He was more interested in the *yaksha*'s strategy for finding her. There didn't seem to be any rhyme or reason to the winding path she was leading them on. Luckily, the tunnels seemed to be used exclusively by *yaksha* slaves. There were no *daitya* anywhere to be seen. The air in the tunnels was damp and the glimmering light from the *mani* stones scanty.

"Do you actually know where you're going?" Dirk asked after a time. Olga didn't hesitate as she took turns, but Dirk saw no rhyme or reason to the route. Finally, they stopped before a tall, arched doorway blocked by criss-crossing metal bars.

"Here," Olga said, with evident satisfaction.

"You mean Pliny and the others are in here?" He stepped up to the bars and looked beyond them. On the other side was a vast empty chamber, a good thirty feet or more in length. Something was inside, something very large that Dirk thought must be a dinosaur. As his eyes grew accustomed to the dark, he saw the thing more clearly.

Then his jaw dropped.

*** 

Anya shook her head. "I don't think I know you anymore, Theo Chalmers."

"They won't be hurt." Chalmers tried to keep from gritting his teeth as he spoke. Convincing people to see things his way had always been his special talent—his superpower, as Pliny called it. Speaking with that tremendous good-natured confidence that said, *everything will be alright—better than alright. I am a learned man of great resources who's read a lot more books than you. Just trust me.* Lately, though, that endless well of confidence had faded.

Anya strolled over to the pile of silken finery laid out for the "guests" to wear. She picked up a carefully folded gown, inspected it, tossed it aside. "Won't they? And you know that how, exactly? Did the great high and mighty Panjandrum of the serpent folk give you his solemn word?"

He had, as it happened, but Chalmers knew better to tell Anya that, because he knew what her response would be, and that it would be correct. The *Naga* lied. They lied whenever it suited them, which was frequently. But it was absurd to paint them as evil monsters; they were so far from humanity that judging them by human standards was a futile exercise.

Still. A liar was a liar, especially where the life of one's granddaughter was concerned. It did his peace of mind no good. Had Anya known the whole truth, and what the *Naga* really had planned for Pliny, her response would be so furious as to endanger them all.

"I'm doing what needs to be done, Anya. I've trained Pliny since she was a child. She'll play her role far better for being unaware of it. She's not helpless."

"She's not a one-woman army either, Theo. Theo, they killed Lenny. They probably killed Hari, and I haven't seen Paul for some time. It's time to stop feeding us half-truths. Will you tell me what it is you're doing down here?"

Sighing, Chalmers turned to face her. The beautiful scientist he had once been in love with still lived in her features. But it had been quite a while since he'd seen love in her eyes.

"They're dying," he said flatly.

"Who? The *Naga*?"

"The *Naga* and the *daitya*. And once they die, rest will follow—the *gryms* and *yaksha* and everything else. It's the sun-stone. It's been lighting and warming this world for millennia, but it's gone sour over time. You saw the lesions and deformities on the *Naga*'s faces, the effect on the *daitya*'s skin color—all that has to do with the radiation from the *mani* stones. That's why the *Nagina* aren't deformed; they keep them down here, away from the light, so the effects of the disease are minimized. And no, I don't have a peer-reviewed paper to prove that. But I've seen the proof, walking before me and talking to me.

"I was their slave, you know. The *Naga*'s. When I first stumbled into this world, I was just another animal to them. They put me to work in the depths of this city. That was how I first came to see what the *mani* stones could do. They extend life, and allow skilled individuals to focus their energies to control lower animals.

"But the stones also kill, over time. I went to the highest *Naga* with my theories—by then, I'd given them that name, after the mythological beings in Indian myth. They didn't believe me— didn't want to, I suspect. They've been down here millions of years, sending parties upworld to keep an eye on their interests and occasionally bring down animals and primitive human species."

"Like the *daitya*...and the *yaksha*," Anya said dully.

Chalmers nodded. "Or their remote ancestors. The *yaksha* are particularly interesting; they don't advertise the fact, but a number of them can speak modern English, or at least make themselves understood in that language. There may have been some interbreeding there, at some point.

"At any rate, when the *daitya* had developed enough, they took over as the *Naga*s' agents on the surface. By then, the *Naga* had weakened; they'd forgotten most of their own technology, including the means by which they'd created the sun-stone that was slowly killing them. When I realized they wouldn't listen to me, I continued my work in secret. By then, I knew how to work with the *mani* crystals, you see. How to change their energies so that they would gradually infect other crystals. A bit like what you'd call a computer virus, I suppose."

"And then you escaped?"

"I did eventually, though it was a near thing. They sent a *thamgrym* after me, a bit like an allosaur with scenting capabilities, rather like a bloodhound. Getting away from it was unpleasant, and I managed to seal up my escape route in the process, but I managed it. My intention was to raise funds to build up a large team, so that I could come back and finish it off. You see how well that went," he added bitterly. "I wasn't without some influence, largely due to my family's money. But in the end, even with your help, I was only able to get together a very small team. At least I was able to seek out and ingratiate myself to the *daitya*. They allowed me to re-establish contact with the *Naga*—not as a slave this time, but as a sort of...a consultant, I suppose you could say. They still don't like me, of course, but they have a very high regard for their own power. They don't see me as a threat, at least.

"And now it's time for the final act. But most of it is out of my hands. You'll be glad to know Hari is still alive, but his role is perhaps the most dangerous of all."

"What do you mean?" Anya asked, narrowing her eyes.

Chalmers cleared his throat. "You see, my idea of the virus wasn't entirely original to me. The *Naga* had a special *mani* crystal they called a 'keystone,' which connected to all the others. I was able to break it into pieces—those are the crystals I gave to each of you before the expedition's start. The *Naga* didn't even realize it was gone. In the interim, I created a replacement that will trigger the final response. I had intended to eventually use the young man—Pliny's bodyguard—as the bearer. As it happened, I had to use Hari."

"God, you really are a bastard," she said. "And don't tell me how noble your intentions were. Those are the biggest bastards, in my view, those with good intentions. What is this 'final response' you're talking about?"

"The activation of my 'virus,' in each and every *mani* stone in Patala. If I'm correct, it will heal the sun-stone and save this world."

"And if you're incorrect?"

Chalmers blew a puff of air between his pursed lips and made a fluttering gesture with the fingers of one hand. *"Boom,"* he whispered.

Anya stared at him in silence for a time. "So you've killed us…or *risked* killing us, which is the same thing as far as I'm concerned…all for the sake of your precious *Naga*."

Chalmers' voice turned pleading. "I can't let them die, Anya. They and their entire world are something amazing, a scientific marvel. Don't you see?"

She didn't punch him, though Chalmers thought that was exactly what she wanted to do. "You could have told me this years ago, when we met," she whispered. "There may have been other options—I may have been able to help you find them. But you didn't. You let good people die, because you wanted to play the great manipulator. I could kill you now...I'd do it happily."

She turned away from him and Chalmers left the chamber. *Staying*, he thought, *would be pointless*. So he didn't see Khresshtra approach Anya once the chamber door had closed, and he didn't see the *Nagina* offer her a long-bladed dagger. Nor did he see Anya take it from her.

Had Chalmers seen her hesitate for an instant before taking the knife, it might have been some comfort to him.

*** 

Hari wasn't sure if Chalmers' disappearance was necessarily a bad thing. He was no longer sure how far he could trust the old man; it wasn't impossible that he was simply waiting for a chance to further betray him.

Besides, he was more interested in the thing in the pit.

He was fairly sure it must be some species of tyrannosaur, but considerably bigger than anything ever found in the fossil record. Hari knew *Giganotosaurus* supposedly dwarfed the *T-rex*, but he had no way of knowing if the thing before him was one or the other. Whatever it was, it showed signs of extensive mutation.

The most noticeable thing about it was its white, blotchy skin, covered with irregular shoals of gleaming multicolored *mani* stones. If it had forearms, they were so tiny as to be mere vestigial lumps. It did not seem to walk so much as drag itself around the floor of the pit. Its huge, unwieldy head turned here and there, seeming to sniff the air, occasionally loosing another of those strangely terrifying infrasound "roars." One eye was abnormally large, rolled up part-way in its head. Where the thing's second eye should have been was blank skin.

A moment later, he realized he didn't need Chalmers to betray him. One of the *daitya* stepped up behind him and, without ceremony, shoved him in the small of the back. It was so much like the scenario he'd imagined earlier that it almost left him unsurprised. The next moment, he was flying face-downward, heading for the floor. The fall didn't last long. Before he was even conscious of it, he felt himself slowing. He had the insane idea that the air had somehow thickened around him, supporting him and cushioning him at the same time. There was a hot, steady throbbing in his chest that could only be coming from the *mani* stone. For once, he was grateful to Chalmers for planting the thing in him.

He dropped slowly past the mutated *T-rex*. The air here smelled yeasty and rancid, but Hari was just as glad the thing had not noticed him, and that he was apparently not to be dashed to pieces at the end of his fall. Once he hit ground, he scrambled for one of the cave entrances, only to realize it was shut up with an elaborate metal gate.

"Hari!" a voice called. It was a male voice, and not Chalmers'—it was far too young. He moved carefully, keeping the wall at his back, until he got to the cave entrance where the voice came from. He recognized the young man Chalmers had engaged as a "guide." A woman was with him, with tousled bronze hair and a kind of reptile-skin bikini. *She looked for all the world like a cartoon cave girl,* Hari thought, *or one of the girls from that prehistoric world movie Hammer had made in the 60s.*

"Dirk, isn't it?" He thrust a hand between the bars for a quick shake, but took care not to take his eyes off the *T-rex* creature for too long. "I don't suppose this thing opens from your end, does it?"

"Hold on," Dirk said, lifting up a stout-looking length of iron. "I don't think it does, but maybe we can do something about that." He shoved the crowbar between the farthest bar and the doorway, and began levering it, trying to get the door open.

"Don't have any idea what that thing is, do you?" Hari was happy the creature didn't appear hungry, but he didn't want to take the situation for granted.

"Little Brother," the cave girl said, not seemingly troubled by anything happening around her. It was hard to tell in the shadowy recesses of the cave, but Hari had the distinct impression she was carelessly examining her nails.

"I *beg* your pardon?"

"Little Brother." She turned to Dirk. "Your *googa*'s *googa*."

Dirk left off levering the door and stared at her. "You mean they're going to try and marry Pliny off to that thing?"

The girl shrugged. Her indifference seemed to give Dirk strength. A moment later, the door cracked and slid open far enough for Hari to slip inside with them.

"What do you mean that's Pliny's *googa*?" Dirk snapped. Something about the prospect plainly rankled him. Hari could hardly blame him, but this was no time for group therapy.

"We should get going," he said. "Wherever it is we're going…"

A moment later, a noise crashed through the pit. *Trumpets*, Hari thought dimly. *Horns*. The *T-rex* didn't appear overly thrilled by the noise. It shook its massive head and roared again.

"Now comes marriage," the cave girl said, sounding bored.

\*\*\*

Pliny stood numbly while Khresshta applied paints to her face. She had chosen silks and clothing at random from the piles made available in their chamber; the *Nagina*'s task was apparently to fine-tune her choices to make her a proper…

"Bride," she whispered. "That's what I am, right? A bride to one of those things." Khresshta's faint smile grew fainter. Pliny was sure she didn't understand her, but she could surely hear the misery in Pliny's voice, and seemed troubled by it.

Monica stood close by, wringing her hands. No attention had been paid to her clothes, which made Pliny feel alternately sorry for and envious of her. Why she had been brought in at all, Pliny wasn't sure, but she was glad she was at her side.

"Your grandfather will do something," Monica said hopefully.

"Will he?" Pliny said dully. "What can he do, exactly? You don't know him, Monnie. If he had anything up his sleeve, he would have tried it by now."

At last, Khresshta lowered her hand, apparently satisfied. Her smile returned and she turned Pliny to face a mirror.

The makeup made her look beautiful and also strange—so strange she might not have been human. The makeup Khresshta had added angles and planes to her features that had not been there before. Her dark hair had been taken out of braids, washed and combed, rebraided, and piled atop her head in an elaborate confection that wouldn't have looked out of place on a Paris runway. The clothes were beautiful, but seemed to reveal as much of her body as they hid.

Two *Naga*s entered the room. Their eyes flickered coldly over Pliny, but they seemed singularly unimpressed. They gestured—not to the girls, but to Khresshtra, who bowed her head and retreated backward.

The *Naga* signaled the girls to follow them. They didn't resist. There seemed no point.

* * *

Chalmers stood on the balcony over the pit, facing the Emperor. That was how he had always translated the chief *Naga*'s title, at least for his own use. The serpent folk had always considered themselves the rulers of the universe, so "king" was much too small a title for the leader.

This *Naga* was not a pleasant sight to look on. He had been affected by the sun-stone's rays more than most of his subjects. Chalmers had an idea this was a matter of pride; the *Naga* were only dimly aware of the damage the sun-stone did, but the Emperor could not allow his own exposure to the damaging rays to be less than his underlings'. As a result, quite a bit of his face consisted of exposed bone and a glistening scar tissue—a kind of surrogate flesh that had grown to replace what he'd lost.

"Little Brother is eager for his wedding day," the Emperor commented, his words made barely comprehensible owing not only to his alien language, but to his lack of lips.

"Yes," Chalmers agreed with a nod, looking down at the mutant dinosaur, which was storming around the bottom of the pit. Something appeared to have agitated the creature. Occasionally, it lowered its head and sniffed at one of the doors. It would then retreat a couple of steps and roar at it, then go back to sniffing. It reminded Chalmers of a dog who sensed a rat behind a closed door. He had an idea what it might have scented…he could only hope he was right.

He had no idea how long "Little Brother" had been in residence in the pit. It—or one much like it—had been there when he had found and been enslaved in Patala. The *Naga*s did not regard it as a god, as he had at first thought, but more a kind of living symbol of their people's rule. The mutations had surely been caused by close proximity to the *mani* stones' energies, just as the *Naga*s' facial deformities had.

Females were "married" to Little Brother from time to time. These were usually *Nagina* of high-ranking families. The *Naga*s would not bestow such an honor on a woman of the *daitya* or— heaven forbid—the *yaksha*, whom they regarded as little better than animals. On very rare occasions, a woman from the upper world would find her way to Patala and become a bride. Such occasions were greatly prized by the *Naga*—they symbolized the snake kings' dominance over the upper world. But that only happened perhaps once or twice in a thousand years.

Something rustled in the entrance to the balcony—it was a soft sound, that of silken skirts rustling about their owners' legs. At first, Chalmers didn't recognize Pliny in the elaborate ceremonial costume. She caught his eye and he saw tears on her cheeks. It made his heart sick.

He knew what would happen, of course. Words would be chanted and she would be thrown to the creature. Her body would lie broken in the floor of the pit and, once Little Brother had noticed her, he would end her sufferings. That, at least, was the *Naga*s' intention. Whether they understood the new bride's connection to Chalmers, he couldn't say. But the Emperor's skull-like grin had an unpleasantly knowing look to it.

Chalmers shut his eyes. He had come here as an ambassador and a seeker of knowledge. Perhaps a savior of sorts. But things had not gone properly. This was his only chance to right them, and he was taking a terrible chance in doing so. He had faith in his granddaughter, but he knew that she and everyone in the world he loved best may have lost all the faith they had in him.

He reached into a pocket and gripped the *mani* stone there. Soon, it would be time to act, and he would only have one chance.

* * *

"They're going to throw her off the balcony," Dirk said dully. They all knew it. "We have to get out there..."

"And do what, exactly?" Hari asked glumly. "Beastie over there won't let us out. Keeping him interested is probably working to prolong Pliny's life as much as anything."

"Yeah, until they throw her down and she breaks her neck."

A moment of silence followed, broken when Hari cleared his throat. "You know, come to think of it...they threw *me* off the balcony, or as good as. And somehow, I..."

A loud shriek rang across the pit, drowning out Hari's words. Little Brother reared up, looking with interest at the balcony, where some kind of struggle was going on.

The angle, as well as the distance, prevented them from seeing clearly. The figures looked tiny, like the miniatures used in war games. The most conspicuous was a plump, pale green thing that put Dirk in mind of a fat grub. It was struggling with a much smaller figure, and more small figures were either scattering out of the way or locked in the struggle with the green thing.

Dirk only had eyes for the smallest of the figures, the one he knew to be Pliny. She was, unsurprisingly, one of those trying to join in the struggle. But the ledge was too narrow, and the *Naga*, whatever their other achievements, had apparently never heard of a safety bar. A pale figure Dirk took to be a *daitya* guard shoved her, and she stood wobbling on the ledge for the briefest of seconds before she toppled off, plummeting for the floor of the pit.

Little Brother reacted to this development with an ear-splitting roar, eagerly charging toward the far wall to claim his bride. The next few moments were dim in Dirk's mind. He cried out and shoved himself against the gate, knocking it open. Then he and Hari were running as fast as they could into the pit, Olga following lackadaisically behind.

*\*\*\**

Chalmers stood on his hands and knees, staring down in horror at the tiny figure plummeting downward. Monica was beside him, holding him and crying, but Chalmers barely noticed her. A moment later, one of the *daitya* guards fell as well, but Chalmers hardly noticed him, either. He was only vaguely aware of the struggle around him. Anya had burst onto the balcony with a dagger in hand and had at once attacked the *Naga* Emperor. She stepped back from him now, the blade dripping in her hand. The creature lay in a bloody heap on the ledge, its grotesque face gasping for breath. Anya seemed unaware of it, and only barely aware of what had just happened to Pliny. Then her eyes focused and with a snarl, she kicked at the creature with one foot. It squealed as it fell off the edge, falling with far greater speed than Pliny had.

A memory flashed through Chalmers' mind of a long-ago summer afternoon at Anya's home in Connecticut, drinking her home-brewed iced tea and smiling together at a young Pliny playing on the floor with plastic dinosaurs. That afternoon, he had thought seriously of inviting her into his life on a more permanent basis...but somehow, his work on behalf of Patala's rulers had gotten in the way, and now it was far, far too late. If he had shown himself to be something less than the man she thought him, she had surprised him as well.

Then one of the *daitya* guards—the fellow who had pushed Pliny off the balcony—came at him, and Anya leapt at him with a sob, shoving the knife into his ribs. That was when Chalmers found the place in his mind that allowed him to work with the crystals.

Activating the *mani* stone was like flipping a switch. It brought a terrible burst of pain. There was also a deep satisfaction, but the pain far outweighed it. He had told himself throughout this whole adventure that Pliny would survive, as though he could will it. But she hadn't, and nothing would ever be the same again. Perhaps he put more effort into the stone as a result.

The last thing he saw was Anya holding him, angrily shouting his name, ordering him to wake up, threatening to kill him if he didn't.

He smiled dimly at her as he left Patala. Good old Anya. She always made everything so *memorable*.

\*\*\*

Dirk swung his crowbar at Little Brother's leg. The edge of it scored a deep wound in the creature's pasty flesh, and it roared, though not as violently as Dirk would have expected. Maybe its nervous system had been affected by the same genetic damage that caused its other deformities. In any case, whatever pain it felt worked to distract it from Pliny, who was now seconds from hitting the pit's floor.

"Aw, Jesus!" Hari yelled. The scientist was several feet away, clutching his head as though he were experiencing the world's worst migraine. Light blazed suddenly out of his chest and then the damnedest thing happened.

Pliny stopped falling.

With maybe a second or two to spare, she froze suddenly, her silks flapping around her like a fairy's gown. She began rising slowly, an almost comical look of amazement on her face. Something big and green hit the pit's floor at about that time, and another something smaller and whiter. The two lay in broken heaps, but Dirk didn't waste time looking at them. He was running with his hands reaching upward, like an idiot, as though he were trying to catch Pliny out of mid-air.

A second later, that was exactly what he did. She grabbed hold of him, burying her face in his shoulder. "Oh God," she whimpered. "Oh God, oh God…"

"I've got you," Dirk said. It sounded idiotic to him, but it was all he could think to say. All he really *wanted* to say. Then suddenly Pliny was swatting at his shoulder and crying for him to turn around, to turn around *now*!

When he managed to obey, he saw Little Brother, much too close for comfort, leaning toward him and snarling…and then suddenly rearing back with an ululating scream, one grotesquely deformed forelimb pawing at a spear suddenly protruding from its side. Several feet away, Olga smiled triumphantly at the creature, making a gesture that was presumably the *yaksha* equivalent of flipping someone off.

Before Little Brother could mount a retaliatory attack, the *mani* stones covering its skin began flashing on and off. Sparks of lightning crackled around it and with a last ear-splitting, faintly defiant roar, Little Brother fell onto its side.

"I don't suppose anyone believes I didn't mean to do that," Hari said. The energy flaring from the stone in his chest was dimming now. He prodded at it, and, wincing, managed to dislodge it, leaving a shallow depression in his skin.

"Feels good to have that off," he muttered.

"We're not done yet," Pliny cried, punching Dirk in the chest. "Anya's up there, and Monica! We've got to get them down! The guards will know something's wrong."

"She's right," Dirk told Hari. "This place'll be swarming with *daitya* in a few minutes. But how do we get up there?"

He was startled by a loud squawk from Olga. The *yaksha* was slowly rising off the pit's floor, her toes kicking in mid-air. Dirk looked to Hari, who was also rising—as was, he noticed suddenly, himself and Pliny.

"Don't look at me, chum," Hari said, laughing. "I'm just along for the ride, same as you." The stone was still sparking and flaring in his hand—*probably expending the last of its energy*, Dirk thought. *Hope it doesn't run out before we get to Anya.*

It was a strange feeling—not being pulled from above but pushed from below, as though something large and soft were being slowly inflated beneath them.

When they had gotten to a height of about twenty feet, a number of pale figures burst into the pit out of several of the gated doorways. These weren't *daitya*, Dirk saw, but the enslaved *yaksha*. The stones in their flesh had gone dark just as Hari's had, and they were whooping and laughing, waving their tools in the air at the slowly rising figures.

"They're free!" Pliny said delightedly. "The stones aren't imprisoning them anymore."

"They've still got the *daitya* to deal with," Dirk pointed out.

"But that doesn't matter! They're free now! They won't let anyone push them around anymore."

"I don't think we have too much to worry about from the *daitya* gang ourselves," Hari put in, turning slow cartwheels in mid-air. "They're free too, you know."

"Grandfather did it," Pliny said happily. "He didn't just discover the world he dreamed of, he freed it."

Dirk nodded, smiling as they continued to rise.

# EPILOGUE

It took some time for the five travelers to reach Tacaraguita. Once they got there, a very disheveled Pliny Chalmers stepped up to the glaring, dark-haired girl at the Grande's desk and cheerfully asked that her and her grandfather's former accommodations be upgraded, so the hotel's entire second floor would be at their disposal. Gabrielle took her time about checking the rooms' availability, but the American girl's money spoke more loudly than her own dislike. Within a few minutes, each of the weary travelers had a room of their own.

The remainder of that day was spent in bathing and sleeping—in that order. The next afternoon, they converged in the dining room for a huge meal, followed by drinks in the memory of those absent.

It had taken Pliny some time to get over her grandfather's death. Anya was distraught as well, and most of the journey home had been made in a gloomy silence, though Hari had been right about their having no trouble from the *daitya*. Whether in celebration of their own freedom or simple disorientation, the pale men had not shown themselves, as they left the *Naga*s' City. Neither had the *Naga*, for that matter.

They had decided to leave and not return. None of them had any taste for bringing Patala and its creatures to the upper world's attention. It seemed enough to know they had accomplished what Chalmers had set out to do.

Once they reached the elevator, Olga had elected to stay behind.

"*Yaksha*," she said, jerking a thumb at her chest. "Don't belong in up-world. Not enough good food."

Before she left, she took Pliny's hand, laying it on top of Dirk's. "*Googa*," she said, in tones of great satisfaction. There had followed quite a bit of blushing and stammering on both Pliny and Dirk's part, until Anya silenced them with a loud snort.

"Old Theo used to say you can't escape destiny. It was one other thing the old goat was right about. So deny it all you like, but get that amulet of yours out, Pliny. 'Good food' is a matter of personal taste, but as for me, I'm hungry for something that wasn't running around on two legs five minutes before."

Now, considerably cleaner and well-rested, they raised their glasses of beer to Theophilus Chalmers.

"*And* to Patala," Hari added. "The city at the bottom of the anthill! I'm glad I saw it...but I'm glad I won't be going back there anytime soon. Though I have to say I'll miss old Hrund, in an odd way. I mean, *very* odd."

"He and his pals won't miss us, I don't think," Anya said. "Besides, they'll have enough on their hands learning to deal with their new world order. I'm just glad whatever Theo managed to do to the stones didn't put their sun out."

At that moment, two men entered the dining room, one tall and lean and glowering, the other short and chubby and cheerful. Both set upon the travelers with loud shouts of pleasure.

"Man, where you *been*?" Juan Pablo cried. "Old Marcus was, what you call, *furious* when you stopped showing up! He said you were his best worker!"

"Well, he's got another career now." Pliny smiled, curling an arm around Dirk's. "We're going back north together, and the first thing I'm going to do is get him in business school. Then we're going to see about opening a guide service. I think it would be an excellent use for my inheritance."

"Looks like wherever you went did you good, Dirk," Luis said approvingly, helping himself to a *saltena* from a large plate on the table. "Got a nice young lady now, a career...it's all looking good for you, man."

"Sure is," Juan Pablo said. A little wistfully, he added, "Did they have more like her wherever you went? She sure is pretty."

"Aw, I had one all set up for you," Dirk said with a smile. "You would have loved her. But she had other plans."

"Story of my life." Juan Pablo sighed, signaling an irritable-looking Gabrielle for a beer. "At least I don't gotta worry about those damn dogs no more."

At that point, Monica rejoined the table, after a trip to the ladies. The tall paleontologist and Juan Pablo smiled at each other with mutual interest.

"And what's your name?" Monica asked. Before Juan Pablo could answer, Anya added, "It isn't *Googa*, by any chance?"

The laughter in the Grande's dining room didn't quiet down for a good half-hour.

END

# CHECK OUT OTHER GREAT DINOSAUR BOOKS

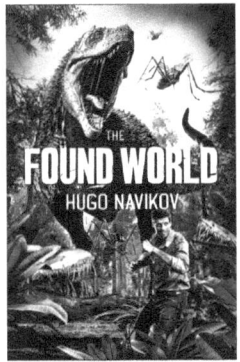

## THE FOUND WORLD
by **Hugo Navikov**

A powerful global cabal wants adventurer Brett Russell to retrieve a superweapon stolen by the scientist who built it. To entice him to travel underneath one of the most dangerous volcanoes on Earth to find the scientist, this shadowy organization will pay him the only thing he cares about: information that will allow him to avenge his family's murder.

But before he can get paid, he and his team must enter an underground hellscape of killer plants, giant insects, terrifying dinosaurs, and an army of other predators never previously seen by man.

At the end of this journey awaits a revelation that could alter the fate of mankind ... if they can make it back from this horrifying found world.

## HOUSE OF THE GODS
by **Davide Mana**

High above the steamy jungle of the Amazon basin, rise the flat plateaus known as the Tepui, the House of the Gods. Lost worlds of unknown beauty, a naturalistic wonder, each an ecology onto itself, shunned by the local tribes for centuries. The House of the Gods was not made for men.

But now, the crew and passengers of a small charter plane are about to find what was hidden for sixty million years.

Lost on an island in the clouds 10.000 feet above the jungle, surrounded by dinosaurs, hunted by mysterious mercenaries, the survivors of Sligo Air flight 001 will quickly learn the only rule of life on Earth: Extinction.

# CHECK OUT OTHER GREAT DINOSAUR BOOKS

## FLIPSIDE
## by JAKE BIBLE

The year is 2046 and dinosaurs are real.

Time bubbles across the world, many as large as one hundred square miles, turn like clockwork, revealing prehistoric landscapes from the Cretaceous Period.

They reveal the Flipside.

Now, thirty years after the first Turn, the clockwork is breaking down as one of the world's powers has decided to exploit the phenomenon for their own gain, possibly destroying everything then and now in the process.

## A MAN OUT OF TIME
## by Christopher Laflan

Five years after the Chinese Axis detonated an unknown weapon of mass destruction off the southern coast of the United States, Special Ops Sergeant John Crider and the members of Shadow Company have finally captured what they all hope will lead to the end of the war. Unfortunately, the population within the United States is no longer sustainable. In an effort to stabilize the economy, the government enacts the Cryonics Act. One hundred years in suspended animation, all debt forgiven, and a chance at a less crowded future are too good to pass up for John and his young daughter.

Except not everything always goes as planned as Sergeant John Crider finds himself pitted against a land of prehistoric monsters genetically resurrected from the fossil record, murderous inhabitants, and a future he never wanted.

# CHECK OUT OTHER GREAT DINOSAUR BOOKS

## PRIMORDIA
## by **Greig Beck**

Ben Cartwright, former soldier, home to mourn the loss of his father stumbles upon cryptic letters from the past between the author, Arthur Conan Doyle and his great, great grandfather who vanished while exploring the Amazon jungle in 1908.

Amazingly, these letters lead Ben to believe that his ancestor's expedition was the basis for Doyle's fantastical tale of a lost world inhabited by long extinct creatures. As Ben digs some more he finds clues to the whereabouts of a lost notebook that might contain a map to a place that is home to creatures that would rewrite everything known about history, biology and evolution.

But other parties now know about the notebook, and will do anything to obtain it. For Ben and his friends, it becomes a race against time and against ruthless rivals.

In the remotest corners of Venezuela, along winding river trails known only to lost tribes, and through near impenetrable jungle, Ben and his novice team find a forbidden place more terrifying and dangerous than anything they could ever have imagined.

## PANGAEA EXILES
## by **Jeff Brackett**

Tried and convicted for his crimes, Sean Barrow is sent into temporal exile—banished to a time so far before recorded history that there is no chance that he, or any other criminal sent back, has any chance of altering history.

Now Sean must find a way to survive more than 200 million years in the past, in a world populated by monstrous creatures that would rend him limb from limb if they got the chance. And that's just his fellow prisoners.

The dinosaurs are almost as bad.